IMPERATOR

THE LAST WITCH OF ROME: BOOK THREE

RHETT GERVAIS

Imperator
The Last Witch of Rome: Book Three

Rhett Gervais
Editor: Paula Grundy
Cover: Jake Caleb, J Caleb Design

Published August 2021
Copyright © 2021 Rhett Gervais

FOLLOW and LIKE:

https://rhettgervais.com/

A SPECIAL OFFER

Building a good relationship with my readers is important to me. I occasionally send newsletters with details about new releases, advanced previews and even the occasional short story. As a bonus if you sign up for the newsletter, you will also receive:

1 - A digital copy of Chosen, the prequel novella to the Last Witch of Rome.

2 - A digital copy of Origin: Children of the Spear: Book One.

3 - A copy of Genesis: Children of the Spear: Book Two.

Just click on the link below and start reading today!

https://rhettgervais.com/new-landing/

P.S I promise, no spam ever!

CONTENTS

PROLOGUE

A CAGED EMPRESS

The piercing roar jolted Lucilla to full wakefulness, her heart pounding out of her chest as she scrambled to the back of her cage, her body stiff and sore from sleeping on the unyielding concrete. She had been in a deep slumber, dreaming of her home on Palatine Hill. Her mind lost in silk sheets and sweet wine of better days, days when she woke in her sumptuous room, enjoying the view from her balcony overlooking the city. Breathing in the sweet smell of orange blossoms from her garden, while her eyes feasted on golden rays of sun dancing off the colorful skyline that was Rome. Another growl from the caged beast across from her brought reality back into sharp focus, pushing away the last remnants of her dream while cementing her firmly into the reality of her dark, dank, and dismal cell.

When the Praetorian guard had thrown her into this terrible place at her brother's orders, she still had hope that he would relent and forget his promise to keep her here forever, but now, after months of loneliness, it appeared, for once, her brother was keeping his word, leaving her with a bitter rage that grew steadily with each passing day.

Casting a wary eye at the pacing lion in the cage across from her, she squinted at faint slivers of sunlight peeking through the wooden partitions that made up part of the Colosseum floor above her, the only sign that morning had come, cursing her with another day toiling under the great amphitheater.

"Good morning, Augusta," said a legionnaire, who entered through her open cell door, not long after she had awoken, spooning a thick gruel from a bucket into a dented pewter bowl and then shoving it into her hands.

"Good to see you, Caius," she said, her mouth watering at the sight of the pale mush in the bowl. "It's been at least a week. I thought you had forgotten us."

"Be grateful we give you anything at all," he said with a grunt, showing her his back while he continued down the corridor, keeping to one side to avoid the lion's outstretched paw reaching at him through the bars. Caius was one of the two legionnaires who were assigned to the hypogeum on days when there were no events. It was clear he despised being among the wretched slaves who were forced to work in the bowels of the Colosseum, but he was a legionnaire and did his duty, regardless of what it was. She had told him who she was during the first few days of her brother's banishment, hoping to curry some favor or a way out of this hell, but he only shrugged as if she had told him the sky was blue. He rarely spoke, but he was better than the man who patrolled the area at night. Far better.

Ignoring the low-throated growl from the cage across from her, she turned her attention to breakfast, which was once again puls, a porridge made from cut wheat and water. Once, when she was a child and refused to eat, her father had made her eat a spoonful as punishment, and she swore she would never be so cruel as to feed puls to anyone, even her own slaves. The porridge was as tasteless as it was innutritious, and she had often thought she would rather starve than eat it, but after a week of having nothing but water, it tasted like a gift from the gods. Squeezing her eyes shut, she dug her fingers into the vile paste, scooping large handfuls into her mouth while pretending it was figs and honey, or sweet sapa spread on thick slices of bread that she had often enjoyed for her morning meal. After a few moments, she frowned in disgust, unable to pretend, no matter how hard she tried. Lucilla opened her eyes and pushed the bowl to one side, saving some of the tasteless gruel for later. Wiping her hands on her once fine stola, the former empress bowed her head in shame, wishing she had the courage to take her own life and end this horrid nightmare.

"You cast aside a gift of food from the gods," said a thin, reedy voice.

Lucilla's head shot up to find a toothless shadow of a man dressed in rags the color of dirt, shambling through the open door of her cell. His long beard was yellow and unkempt, and his jaw moved constantly while his bulging gray eyes stared hungrily at the bowl of puls. "The gods have abandoned me," she said without thinking, echoing her deepest thoughts.

"Then you should be punished," he said, taking a step closer. "Left to starve like the rest of us!"

She recoiled when a whiff of his odor assaulted her nostrils, covering her nose in a futile attempt to block out the smell of urine and old sweat "Don't come any closer," she said, using the bars to push herself up. In her months here, Lucilla had mostly kept to herself, working in silence at mundane tasks assigned to her. The other slaves had done the same, most of them too broken or despondent to bother anyone. Given her once fine dress and fair skin, it was clear to everyone that she had never worked a day in her life under the blazing hot sun, and for the most part, they considered her an ill omen, best to be avoided. They spoke to her only when necessary, and thus far, no one had dared to enter her space.

"And who would stop me," he scoffed, offering her a toothless grin as he came closer. "The gods have abandoned you."

"It's mine!" she said, holding the dented bowl in a white-knuckled grip before he could get to it. "You can't just take it!"

"You look like you've never been hungry a day in your life," he said, his tongue sticking out to wet his lips. "Lots of meat still on your bones."

Lucilla put the bowel of porridge on the floor behind her and faced him fully, adrenaline and anger pushing back weeks of hunger. "Take another step and it will be your last."

The filthy man sneered, shambling toward her, roughly trying to push her aside in a desperate attempt to get to the tasteless gruel. "I can do whatever I want, when I want."

His words struck her like a charging beast. Commodus had spoken the same words to her, months ago in the baths. Felix had sacrificed his life to keep her safe, But today she had no one. "No!" she screamed. "It's mine! Get out! Get out!" The filthy man was taller than her, but he was right, Lucilla had more meat on her bones, and when they both crashed into one another, she realized he was nothing more than skin and bones. Pushing back at him with months of unspent rage, she drove him out of her cell, expelling every moment of abandonment, of betrayal, of hurt on his bony body.

They came to a jarring halt with a hollow clang when they slammed against the iron bars of the lion's cell, and she came back to herself when his eyes shot open, a titanic roar sending her reeling back on her haunches in terror. Lucilla's jaw fell open as the lion stood on its rear legs, taller than a man, while its front claws dug deep into the man's flanks.

"Domina, please," he screeched, reaching for her with a trembling hand as the lion's sharp claws tore at his belly, staining his filthy rags with bright blood.

She lurched forward to help him, her first impulse to save his life, but then she clutched her hand to her breast, raising her chin while showing him a cold smile. "You just said you can do whatever you want, when you want. Well, make the beast stop. I don't care either way." Without another word, Lucilla turned her back to him, ignoring his weakening screams while returning to her cell and sitting cross-legged, slowly eating her porridge while she watched him die, unfazed by the sound of tearing flesh and cracking bone.

When Caius returned not long after, his face paled when he saw the lion hovering protectively over the remains of its meal. "What happened here?"

"One less mouth to feed," she said with a shrug. The legionnaire opened his mouth to protest, when suddenly he crumpled in a heap, falling without as much as a groan.

"When they told me what he had done to you," said a dark silhouette, who appeared over him, wiping his bone dagger on the dead man's red legionary cloak, "I did not expect for you to survive beyond a few days."

Lucilla tensed, wiping her hands on her filthy stola as she stood. "By the gods," she whispered, grabbing her empty dish and holding it in front of her like a shield.

A thin man dressed in a fine tunic and an expertly wrapped purple toga stepped into view, and she gasped when she saw that his face was concealed by a red painted human skull, decorated with garish yellow teeth. "Don't fear, I come as an ally," he said, returning the blade to a leather sheath on his hip.

"I know who you are," she scoffed. "Vesper and Narcissus told me of you. You're some Sandawei savage playing at being a proper Roman."

"Your little Ose witch knows nothing," he said, his hollow voice dripping with hatred, "and her sheep lover is little better."

Lucilla raised her chin, a smile coming to her face, knowing she had touched a nerve. "Well, the pair of them have killed every one of your people that the gods have put along a path, so I will believe them before you."

"Well, they are not here to help you now... are they?"

"You stand in the blood of a man I killed today... and I have been trapped down here long enough to know that I am ready to die, so do what you will."

"Well then, I see that you have no desire to be free," he began, turning to leave, "and that I've wasted my time."

"Wait!" she said, licking her lips. "What do you want?"

"That's better," he said, facing her once more. "As to what I want, well, I want you."

Lucilla's fine brows narrowed, and she shook her head. "I am a loyal citizen of Rome and have no desire to ally myself with her enemies."

He adjusted his toga, holding it up so it wouldn't be soiled by the pool of blood growing at his feet. "The empire has not been loyal to you. In fact, now that your brother has done exactly what he promised, the people of Rome consider you to be a traitor, allied with those who tried to kill the emperor. They think you have been banished and have all but forgotten you."

"My husband will find me," she began, her hands gripping tightly to the front of her stained stola, "and I'm sure Vesper and Narcissus are looking for me."

"Oh, they looked for a time," he said in an amused tone, "but they assumed that Commodus had you executed, and they have long abandoned the search."

"Liar! How would you know anything!" she shot back, her nostrils flaring while hope fled from her heart.

"Little happens in Rome that I don't know about. I have eyes everywhere."

She looked away, biting the inside of her cheek so she wouldn't scream. Lucilla had hoped that by some miracle, Vesper would find her, that somehow with some trick or incantation, she would awaken one moment with the Ose woman taking her home. But if the masked Sandawei were telling the truth, if the world had forgotten her, she was not sure how many more days she could take toiling away like this. "I will not betray an empire I have spent my life serving, even if it has abandoned me."

"I won't ask you to betray the empire," he said. "I only ask that you help me remove your brother's head."

"Commodus? Why?" The moment the words spilled from her lips; Lucilla regretted it. She owed her brother nothing. He was the reason she was trapped here, and she had often spent the hours of her days dreaming of ways to murder him.

"For the same reason you and your allies tried. For the same reason others have tried," he said. "Your brother is too dangerous to be left alive."

"I will not kill my brother just so some barbarian enemy from Africa Proconsularis can take his place. You savages will not rule Rome, not while I live."

A hollow laugh echoed from behind his mask, and his slim form shook with glee. "Oh no, my dear, I have no desire for that. No, the person we intend to rule Rome has the best claim to be imperator. She is the wife of a former emperor, daughter to another, and since your brother has no legal heir..."

"She would have the best claim to the title of imperator and pontifex maximus," she finished for him, her voice barely a whisper. "Me?"

"Yes," he said, nodding to her. "Augusta, not just in title, but in power! All you have to do... is take my hand, and all you desire will be yours."

"What must I do?" asked Lucilla, all thoughts of resistance forgotten.

"You must make a bargain," he said, his voice full of amusement.

"Here... Now? In this horrid place, with you?"

"No, you must meet the matron," he said, offering his hand. "She will set you on the path to true power."

Lucilla glanced around the dank cell, hesitating for only a heartbeat before she took his outstretched hand. "Then let it be done. Take me away from this place... and we will see if this matron has the power to do as you say!"

ONE
OSTIA

The storm rolled in off the ocean, wild and wicked, blinding her with bright flashes of lightning, while booming peals of thunder reverberated across the night sky. She raised her hood to cover her braided hair, the meager wool garment offering little protection from the pelting rain that stung her dark skin.

Vesper was grateful for the rain; it washed away the cloying smell of tar and stale fish that permeated the port, clearing the trash-filled streets of the riffraff, who scurried like rats to avoid the storm, leaving her alone in the nighttime streets. In the distance, she caught sight of a crudely painted sign of a crab holding a cup of wine, and she reached out through the bond she shared with Narcissus, sensing that he was close, and growing closer. They had spent the evening searching for this pompina, and she was grateful to have at last found it, having little taste for the port of Rome.

Vesper jogged the final leg through the dark streets, elbowing past the sailors seeking shelter from the rain to enter the well-lit room that filled with swaying men and women, who danced and sang at the top of their lungs, lost in the joys of wine and ale, while filling their bellies with their daily bread. Spotting the man she was looking for,

Vesper ducked under a staggering woman whose sweat-stained stola clung to her like a second skin, making her way to a low stone table, where a barrel-chested man in a salt-stained coat stared into his cup, oblivious to the cloying heat of the packed pompina.

Without waiting for permission, she settled in across from him, wiping away the sweat rolling down her brow. The man's clothes, weathered skin, and greasy, thinning hair painted the picture of a man who had spent his life on the sea, and even from across the table she could smell the spray of the ocean on him. His red bulbous nose made it clear he spent a great deal of time lost in wine... so much so that he didn't immediately notice her.

She was about to shake him when he snapped to attention, his weary eyes drilling directly into her. "Unless you plan to pay for my drink, it would be best that you leave my table... before I make you leave," he said in a voice that was rough and harsh.

"Apologies," said Vesper, throwing a few coins on the table. "I will pay for your wine and your time, of course. I was told that if I needed to find someone, you were the man."

"That was a long time ago," he said, rubbing his hand through a patch of greasy hair that clung to his skull. "I'm just an old navigator for hire now, nothing more."

"She said you always say that. She also said nothing happens in the port that Isídōros don't know about."

"Isídōros!?" he scoffed, rolling his eyes. "It's just Isi now, plain, simple Isi. Whoever gave you that name is playing you for a fool. You should leave. Now!" Glaring at her in silence, the old sailor made his meaning clear, shifting in his seat to show a dagger under his coat.

"Please. I'm looking for a friend," said Vesper, speaking quickly. "A woman. She's been missing for months: anything you could tell—"

"I said leave!" he said, standing up on shaking legs, fingering the hilt of the dagger, his meaning clear. "Tell whatever idiot that gave you my name—"

Vesper shook her head, crossing her arms over her breasts. "She said you would say that too."

"What do you mean? Who gave you my name?"

"Hello, Isídōros," said her mother, appearing from behind him, draping an arm over his shoulder, showing him a brilliant smile. "Where's my boat!?"

"By the gods! Lillith!" he said, his eyes shooting open as he plopped back to his seat, clutching at his chest as if he'd seen a ghost.

Her mother laughed as she came around the table, her eyes never leaving his as she slid in beside Vesper on the stone bench, waving a serving woman over as she showed the whites of her teeth to the sputtering sailor. "Bring us some wine sweetened with sapa," she began when the serving woman arrived. "Make it two cups for my friend here, before he chokes on his own tongue."

"It's just Isi now... and you're supposed to be dead," he said, catching his breath while his jaw hung open.

"I was," said Lillith, "but the lords of the underworld let me go. Just so I could collect the debts you owe me!"

"The boat sank," he sputtered, his eyes wide with worry. "Years ago... crashed upon the rocks. I almost died."

"Well, we stole that boat together," said her mother, putting her hands flat on the table as she locked eyes with him. "You owe me at least half of everything you earned over the years. That was the deal! I'm sure you did the wise thing and put my share aside... right?"

"Quintis told me you were dead," he squealed as if it explained everything, his voice full of terror. "And there were expenses... but I'll find some way to pay you back. I swear!"

"I know you, Isi," said Lillith, crossing her arms. "I would bet that my money was squandered away on dice, wine, and women... and a lot of wine."

"There was the occasional toss... and, of course, a bit of wine but—"

Vesper raised a hand to cover her smile, enjoying how her mother made the poor man squirm, but after it was clear that he had nothing to offer, she leaned in close to her mother. "What's the point of this?

Clearly the poor man doesn't have more than a few denarii to his name, much less a boat—"

"The best debts are those that cannot be repaid," said Lillith with a wink, returning her attention to Isi. "If you cannot pay me what you owe, then I am within my rights to sell you at the slave market. I won't get much but—"

"No," he pleaded, his eyes darting back and forth between them. "That would be the end of me. Please, Lillith, I'll do anything."

"Anything?" said Lillith, frowning at him. "Brave words. Tell me what you know. I'll decide if you're worth my time?"

The serving woman arrived, and Isi threw her a grateful look as he drank deep, blood-colored wine spilling down his chin before he continued. "I will tell you what I know," he said in a rush. "I still have a few old contacts in the legionary. Who are you looking for?"

Lillith pointed at Vesper with her chin, and Isi gave her the same expectant look. "We're looking for a highborn woman," began Vesper, glancing around the pompina to make sure no one was listening. "Pale with fine features, brown hair, usually coiffed, but—"

"You're describing half of the patrician women in Rome," he scoffed, scratching his thinning hair.

Vesper pressed her lips together, trying to decide how much to tell the man. "You would know her if you'd seen her," she said at last, reaching into her pouch to fish out a few hammered silver denarii and handing them to him.

"I don't understand," said Isi, weighing the coin in his hand.

"The woman on the coin," said Lillith. "She is the one we are searching for."

The old sailor paled beneath his weathered skin, and he dropped the coins as if they burned his hands. "The emperor's sister?" he rasped, his eyes darting in all directions. "She's been banished, of course. Everyone knows that. Commanded to spend the rest of her days away from Rome on some country estate."

"That's a lie, and you know it, Isi," said her mother. "I can see it on your ugly face. Tell me what you know, or I will see to it that you are sold to the sanitation department. You can spend the rest of your life up to your waist in sewage."

Isi shook his head, squeezing his eyes shut. "Please, Lillith, you don't know what you're asking. Things in the city are different now; everyone is afraid! People are disappearing. Not just slaves and plebeians, but highborn patricians too."

"How long has this been going on?" asked Vesper.

"Months now," said Isi, taking another sip of wine, "but it grew worse after the attack in the western market."

Her mother gave Vesper a worried look before moving from her seat to slip in beside the old sailor, draping an arm over his shoulder. "Calm down, Isi. Tell me what you know of Lucilla, and I will keep you safe. Just like the old days."

He wiped sweat from his forehead, offering her a toothless smile. "On your word?"

"Of course, Isi," said Lillith. "Just like the old days."

He took another deep draft of wine and then nodded. "From what I know, she never left the city," he said, his shoulders slumping in defeat. "That's all I know. I swear it."

"Who would know more?" asked Lillith.

"I don't know. My old network is gone for the most part; my contacts are all retired or dead."

"Don't lie to me, Isi. I find it hard to believe that the frumentarii, who served two former emperors, knows nothing of the happenings in his city," said Lillith.

"Frumentarii?" asked Vesper, casting a curious glance at Isi.

"Why do you think we're talking to him? Isi here was a spy back in his day, posing as a simple sailor so that he could ferret out the enemies of Rome," said Lillith in mocking tones.

"You never respected what we did, Lillith," said Isi, frowning into his wine cup.

"Bah, why waste time with all that sneaking around when you can just bury a blade in a man's belly. Let the gods sort it all out later."

"It doesn't matter anymore. Commodus ordered all of us who served in fettering out secrets, to retirement," he said, looking over his shoulder. "With many of us suffering fatal accidents not long after we were dismissed."

"Then tell me who would know," said Lillith.

Vesper listened in fascination while Isi rambled off a list of names to her mother, his face growing wearier the longer he spoke. Vesper was about to pull her away from the hapless sailor, when she felt a surge of panic flow from the bond she shared with Narcissus, and she looked up to see his bright red hair and pale face at the door of the pompina, standing head and shoulders above the other patrons. At first, she wondered what he was going on about, but then seeing him give the signal, she knew their time was up. "Mother, we have to go," she said, scanning for an exit as Narcissus pushed his way through the crowd while glancing constantly over his shoulder.

"Legionnaires from the city guard, a dozen cohorts or so," he said, answering her question before she asked. "I don't think I was spotted, but they are sweeping across the square, looking for escaped slaves would be my guess." Vesper rose to her feet, pressing her lips together in worry. Hundreds of slaves had escaped in the revolt months ago, she and Narcissus included. But over time, many had been recaptured or killed, as the common slaves had nowhere to go and made the mistake of trying to hide in the very city that had held them in chains.

"There is a way out the back into the alley," said Lillith, grasping Isi by his arm, "Come on, you're with us, just to be safe."

"I am a free man," protested the old sailor, clutching the table as he rose unsteadily to his feet. "I don't want to be caught up in any of this business."

"Too late for that," said Narcissus, eyeing the old sailor while clearing a path through the throng, bursting into a garbage-strewn alley in back of the pompina, Vesper cursing when they found the path leading to the street blocked by legionnaires.

"If we surrender, perhaps they will show mercy," said Isi, starting to raise his hands.

"The legion is not known for its mercy. I have no intention of surrendering to them," said Vesper, nodding to Narcissus before continuing. "We do this the new way, like we practiced"

The big Celt showed her a feral grin, slapping his meaty palms together. "I've been wanting to try this!"

Vesper's grin matched his as she opened herself to the weave, shuddering with pleasure as torrents of clean Ase poured through her body, sending gooseflesh up and down her arms. The port city was far from Rome's vile corruption, and as such, the weave here was not tainted, and she was able to draw on its power instead of relying only on her own limited power. The concentric patterns decorating her arms flashed a bright white when she raised her arms over her head while singing an ancient Ose chant, and a moment later, a wild maelstrom of cool air descended on the alley, with heavy gusts of wind kicking up dust, debris, and garbage, obscuring them from sight for just an instant and blinding the legionnaires. Then, continuing her song under her breath, she called on the knowledge she had gleaned from Eshu, tapping into the wisdom of the ancient loa. With a flick of her wrist, she banished the blinding dust and debris, and once the air was cleared, the legionnaires as a group fell back, drawing their weapons and raising their massive shields as they suddenly faced off against not one, but six massive Celts who all resembled Narcissus.

"I see you are putting Eshu's teaching to good use, Daughter," said Lillith, nodding with approval as the copies of the big Celt crept forward.

Vesper smiled with glee at her new skill of the weave. Reality fought back when the impossible happened, so Vesper did the next best thing, concealing her manipulations in ways that were simple to explain: dust, wind, and debris, all abundant in the filth of Rome. Narcissus and the copies of him charged the confused legionnaires who, despite their wide-eyed panic, followed their training, locking their shields together in an impenetrable phalanx, bracing against the onslaught of charging flesh and heavy blows.

Most soldiers would have panicked and lost their nerve when a small army of titans crashed into their midst, but the legionnaires held with rock-steady discipline, bracing themselves so the heavy bodies slamming into their shields had little effect beyond pushing them back. Then as one shouted, their voices echoing in the alley, "Push!" As one, the legionnaires heaved back with all their might, staggering the copies of the big Celt for a heartbeat. Then, suddenly, their shields were turned to the side, the phalanx opened as they struck as one, spears and javelins plunging into her small army of Celts, the doppelgängers falling back and then vanishing in a cascade of blinding, multicolored lights.

The legionnaires were about to close ranks once more when Vesper and Narcissus appeared in their midst, the big Celts' long arms and meaty fists delivering one titanic blow after another, shattering noses and knocking the hapless men to unconsciousness. Vesper was more subtle, using the hilt of her gladius to do the same.

"Why not kill them?" said Lillith, eyeing the pair's handiwork, a distasteful frown on her beautiful face.

"I will not kill men for simply doing their duty," said Vesper, locking eyes with her mother.

Her mother shook her head. "I would not have shown them such mercy, and they certainly would have not given us any quarter."

"Then they are lucky we don't think in such ways," growled Narcissus, stepping protectively in front of Vesper. "How many times does she have to explain that to you."

Lillith opened her mouth to protest when Vesper silenced her with a look. "Enough! Narcissus is right. Now, let's move. We've attracted enough attention as it is." Vesper showed her mother her back, turning just in time to find a blade falling toward her head. By instinct, she jumped back, the blade whistling past her face by a hairsbreadth.

She staggered into Narcissus, her heart leaping to her throat when she looked her attacker up and down. He was small and compact, no taller than her, with tight-knit curls and dark eyes that never seemed to blink. What shook her was the realization that his dark skin were covered in geometric patterns similar to her own, and just under the leather vest, she caught hints of something tattooed onto his chest. Vesper opened her mouth to speak when, to her amazement, the patterns on his arms began to glow, and he pointed a heavy, bladed weapon at her. "Vesper, daughter of Abeo. You are in possession of stolen power: return it or face the great loa's justice!"

TWO

THE MATRON

When she had taken the red-masked Sandawei's hand, Lucilla had expected it to be a simple gesture of agreement, but the instant their flesh touched, what little light around them dimmed, and a cold wind blew over her, raising gooseflesh up and down her arms. Her nose hairs froze as she drew in an icy breath, her jaw falling open when she realized that the hypogeum was gone, and they were somewhere else, somewhere dark where even the sound of her breathing was muted and far away.

"Follow... and don't dare leave the path," said the red-masked Sandawei, frosted breath coiling like smoke around the edges of his garish skull.

"Where are we?" asked Lucilla with a whisper, glancing down to see they were standing on a strange cobblestone path that vanished off into the distance over a small hill in one direction, and descending off into darkness in the other.

"A place forgotten by the world... where even the gods cannot see," he said, speaking as if by rote. Without another word, he set off in the direction of the small hill, dragging her along behind him.

Lucilla glanced around, trying to find her bearings but she could see little in the cloying darkness, and after a few moments she gave up, pulling her hand away roughly from his grip. "I am not a child," she said, stopping in place. "I can follow without being dragged about."

He turned to face her, his eyes behind the mask twinkling in amusement. "That's exactly what a child would say," he mocked, shaking his head.

Lucilla pushed out her lower lip, cursing herself when she realized he was right. "A-pologies," she said, "But I don't need you to hold my hand. I will stay close."

With a shrug, he turned, waving for her to follow, "Very well. Just do as you're told. It would not be pleasant for you beyond the path."

She nodded, swallowing harsh words while she matched his brisk pace. They had been following the path for long enough that she had lost all sense of time, when a distant whisper reached her ear, subtle and soft at first, but quickly growing into a cacophony that staggered her. She put her hands to her ears trying to block it out, when a familiar voice called her name, "Lucius!" she shouted, clutching her chest.

"What?" said the masked Sandawei, stopping to look at her.

"L-Lucius," she whispered, staring hard into the darkness. "My husband!" Lucilla took a step forward, drawn to the voice of the first man who had treated her as an equal and not just some prize to be won. A man who could make her laugh at the worst of times and cry with joy during the best, who had been taken away from her heart too soon, struck down in the prime of his life.

Before she could take a step off the path, Lucilla found herself pulled back violently, wincing from pain in her bottom as she was hurled onto the cobblestone path. "Your husband is long dead," said the Sandawei, towering over her, "and you will be, too, if you step into the darkness."

"Lucius would never hurt me," she said, her voice hitching up with desperation. "If I could just talk to him... one last time, to say goodbye."

"The man you knew is long gone," he began in a soft voice, gazing out at the darkness. "The thing that is calling to you is little more than a shade of what he once was, forgotten by the gods. It is desperate for a taste of life... your life, if you're foolish enough to follow it."

"But—"

"It will devour all that you are," he continued, crouching down and meeting her gaze, "leaving you an empty shell... just like *he* is now."

Lucilla hugged herself, rocking back and forth. "Surely something must remain?"

"Those that are cast into this place have been punished, cursed for some mortal sin. Even we Sandawei, at times imprison the worst of us here, trap them for all eternity in torment. You must forget him."

Staring into his eyes, Lucilla could see hints of pain, that he was telling the truth. "You've lost someone to them."

The masked man gave her an unblinking stare before nodding ever so subtly. "My mother," he said, rising to his feet while dry-washing his hands. "She was weak, a foolish Roman woman, who could not endure the call of her ancestors."

"Your mother was Roman?" asked Lucilla.

"We aren't far from our destination," he said, changing the subject. "It would be best that we not linger here too long."

"Is she out there?" pressed Lucilla, starting to understand the nature of this place. "Is it her voice that calls to you, just like my Lucius?"

The Sandawei grunted, adjusting his toga that was dragging along the cobblestone path. "Yes," he said at last, his voice croaking.

A chill ran down her spine when something in the inflection of his voice seemed vaguely familiar, and she realized that this was not some stranger standing before her. She knew him: how, she couldn't be sure, but she was certain of it. "You have my sympathies," she said at last, coughing to cover her hesitation.

He leaned forward and raised a thin hand as if he were about to lash out, his eyes wide with anger, only to hesitate when Lucilla raised her chin defiantly, daring him to hit her. After a moment, he leaned back, offering a hand to help her up. "Apologies, offering sympathy, is often an insult among my people. A sign that a person is weak and in need of... comforting."

"Then we will make for strange bedfellows," she said, taking his hand while hunting for any hints of familiarity in his eyes.

"Well said."

They walked on in silence for a time, with only the whispers of the dead for company, and Lucilla was about to ask how much longer that they would be in this horrid place, when the cobblestone and cloying darkness gave way to a loose gravel pathway, the sky growing lighter as they made their way through an overgrown garden that smelled of orange blossom and jasmine. "Where are we?" she asked, catching glimpses of white marble and fire-hardened brick buildings just beyond the high trees along their path.

The red-masked Sandawei stopped to adjust his toga while squaring his shoulders. "It would be best that you not know, not that you would believe me if I told you," he said, shaking his head. "Now, the matron whom you are meant to meet is just ahead. Show her proper respect, remain calm, and above all, do not lie to her. If you can do that, she will set you on the path to ruling this empire."

"I would laugh if I wasn't so terrified," she said, following his lead and adjusting her stola as best she could despite the filth and grime that covered the garment.

They entered a clearing, and Lucilla's hackles rose when she was struck by the familiar odor she had come to associate with the Sandawei, the sickly stench of rotting meat that had been left out too long in the summer sun. She prepared herself to meet some vicious Sandawei warrior, or a corrupt vodun, like Saoterus. Instead, in the heart of the clearing was a woman dressed in the modest fashion typical of a Roman matron, wearing a woolen stola that fell past her knees and a brightly patterned palla that covered her exposed shoulders. She had caramel-colored skin and deep lines etched around her eyes and mouth that creased into a smile when she and the masked man entered the clearing. Lucilla raised her eyebrows in amusement when the older woman ignored them, focusing her attention on a dull gray piece of wool she was knitting, her hands a blur as she deftly tucked and looped the string with a pair of bone-white needles. Lucilla knew the game well and had done the same herself many times. Doing some mundane task while forcing those beneath you to wait, making rank and position clear.

"You are patient," said the matron at last, meeting her gaze with eyes that were a bright amber. "That is good... a sign of strength." The moment their eyes met, Lucilla's stomach clenched, and she bit the inside of her cheek to control her fear. She could not be sure if it was the smell of death, or the odd shade of her eyes, but Lucilla was certain something about the woman was unnatural, inhuman.

"Clearly a trait we share," said Lucilla, eyeing the small beads woven into the matron's braided hair, pressing her lips together when saw that they were not just bits of stone, but carved bones made to resemble tiny skulls. "Your people have been very patient, growing in our fine city while we remain oblivious to your presence."

The matron frowned at the man in the red mask, shaking her head at him. "Patience is a powerful tool, a tool that Kubwa here has forgotten in his thirst for power."

The man in the red mask sucked in a hollow breath, his eyes going wide. "Matron!"

"Don't worry, boy," she said with a dismissive wave. "No one in Rome knows your true name. This one least of all."

"She is not a fool," began Kubwa, his voice full of anger behind the garish mask.

"No, she is not," said the matron, shifting aside on the bench and motioning for Lucilla to sit, "and your outburst will only give her hints to the truth. Now leave us, before I decide that you should face the final death now that I have her."

Kubwa stiffened, balling his fists at his sides. "Very well, I will wait for your—"

"That will not be necessary. Return home and keep from sight. You've done enough damage in these last few months."

Lucilla cocked her head, fascinated as he turned on his heel and returned the way they came, the light passing through him as he faded from sight until finally vanishing as if he had never existed. When he was gone, Lucilla turned to the matron, offering a tight-lipped smile while raising her chin. "I am Annia Aurelia Galeria Lucilla, daughter to Emperor Marcus Aurelius, Augusta, and wife to Lucius Verus. Know that I will never betray Rome or her people. I only speak with you because I fear my brother is a danger to the empire, and the world."

The matron's face lit up with a smile, deepening the fine lines around her mouth. "I am known as Mother Ayaba, leader of the Sandawei people in the empire, and for the moment we have a common enemy, one that is in our best interests to have removed from this world."

"Then we are in agreement," said Lucilla. "What do you want from me? What is your price to make me Augusta?"

The older woman sniffed, folding her hands in her lap. "Straight to business. Well then, you must be willing to make sacrifices, do things that will shift the balance of power in the world."

"Rome will not bow to anyone," she said, "nor will I."

"I would never ask such a thing," said Mother Ayaba. "You may have your empire. Keep what is yours, but your expansion on the great continent shall cease; you will leave the garden of life to the Sandawei."

"The garden of life?" asked Lucilla, leaning away.

"What you call Africa Proconsularis," she said, sniffing in disdain. "We know the garden of life, the crucible where the great god Olodumare birthed every living thing. It was gifted to the Sandawei at the beginning of time. It was taken from us. We want it back. Once it is ours again, we will not let any other soul upon its shores."

The more she spoke, the more Lucilla found herself nodding along in agreement with the matron's every word, lost in her amber gaze, mesmerized by her warm smile, a sense of calm washing over her the longer the kindly older woman spoke. "Then what would you have me do to begin?" she asked in a flat tone.

"The senate," said the matron. "They have the wealth and power we need. We need only convince them of our plans, gain their support, and the empire is yours."

"Senator Magnus tried as much," said Lucilla with a frown. "It did not go well for him. He almost lost his life... and is still in hiding."

"The scrawny man was a fool, lacking the birthright and charisma you possess in spades, Augusta."

At the mention of her old title, a wide grin spread across her face while her blood raced with excitement. "It can be done," said Lucilla. "We will have to meet with the senators in secret, convince them of need for a change."

"We will meet them together," said Mother Ayaba, her smile growing wider, "Make them see that you are the best person to succeed your brother."

"A wise plan," said Lucilla, plans already forming in her mind.

Mother Ayaba offered her hand, nodding that Lucilla take it. "We are allies, then, sworn to end the life of Commodus."

Lucilla was about to take the other woman's hand in confidence, when a whiff of rot touched her nostrils, and something in her snapped, like a mirage of an oasis fading away when you came to close. The garden, Mother Ayaba were nothing but an illusion, and she could see what was really there. Beneath the overgrown plants were piles of scattered bones, knee deep in some places, gnawed and cracked with the marrow sucked out. The kindly matron's face was a ghastly skull with yellowed teeth, her aged skin paper thin and haggard. In that moment, Lucilla knew that every word was a lie, that she was being drawn into part of some great deceit.

"Are you listening to me?" asked Mother Ayaba.

Lucilla's attention snapped back to the matron, swallowing to wet her dry throat. "Yes, of course," she lied, showing her the whites of her teeth. "I was lost in thought of how I could better the lives of the Roman people."

Mother Ayaba smiled like a hyena sizing up its prey. "Of course, Augusta," she said smoothly, using Lucilla's ancient title. "You will be a wise leader, one that shall take Rome to greater heights. With my help, of course."

"With your help," repeated Lucilla, parroting the treacherous Sandawei's words. Without another word, she took Mother Ayaba's hand, keeping her features still when she took it. There was more going on here than Lucilla could see; the Sandawei leader had plans that she needed her for, and if Lucilla wanted to find them out, she would have to play along for now. It was a dangerous game, but one Lucilla had played her entire life. She only prayed to the gods she had the will to endure, so that Rome could endure.

THREE
DISTANT RELATIONS

"Wait!" shouted Vesper, holding up a shaking hand, her jaw hanging open in awe. "You're Ose, chosen... like me," she said, eyeing features similar to her own yet somehow different. The geometric patterns on his arms resembled her own but twisted and bent in odd ways, leading to a heart rune hidden under his vest, maybe a baobab or something else entirely. Of what, she couldn't be sure, but she was desperate to find out.

Her attacker stepped back, spinning a heavy blade that was engraved with odd patterns that drank in the light. Narrowing his eyes, he glared at the patterns on her arms. "Chosen, yes," he said in a baritone voice, "but not like you! I am no thief." With a deep growl, he came at her, spinning the heavy, flat blade in wide circles to drive her back. Vesper summoned a gladius by habit, her gleaming blade sparking against his when she parried a tight swing. Through her bond with Narcissus, she felt him adjust his stance, pivoting to switch places with her, and instinctively, she danced to her right, concealing the big man's movement as he lashed out with a vicious hook that should have removed her attacker's head. Instead, the big Celt caught only air, stumbling, catching himself at the last moment so he didn't land on his face.

"Eshu's tricks won't help you," said her attacker, appearing behind her, blocking a quick jab from Lillith that kept him severing Narcissus's spine. Moving like a hunting cat, he spun, his boot catching her mother under the chin, sending her reeling.

Vesper's stomach clenched when he came at her again, vanishing and reappearing, slipping in and out of existence with every step, his bizarre movement throwing her off guard. "I have stolen nothing," she said, turning away a thrust aimed for her heart, only to gasp when he reversed his grip, his elbow catching her on the bridge of her nose and snapping her head back.

"You serve the deceiver," he said, drawing back to stab her, only to vanish when Narcissus caught his sword arm.

"Where did he go?" snarled the big Celt, bristling with rage while he scanned the alleyway.

"He travels the filaments," said Lillith, holding her gladius up in front of her. "Using the weave to leap from place to place."

Vesper matched her mother's defensive stance, waiting, watching for their attacker to come at them again. "I've done that, but I didn't know you could make such short jumps, to use it in battle."

"It is a rare talent," said Lillith, licking her lips. "One that I have only read about in ancient texts."

Nodding at her, Vesper shifted her vision to see the world of the weave, observing the infinite number of connections that branched out from their small group, connections that touched every living thing in the world, making up what they called reality. "I thought there were no more Ose," she said, taking a quick glance at her mother. "No djambe, no more chosen." Before Lillith could respond, the stranger appeared again, his heavy blade falling toward her head. Vesper wrenched her body, twisting to block the wicked cut with her gladius, only to curse when he vanished just as their blades would have connected, and then appearing behind her, about to cut her down. She was shocked when a jolt of pain shot, not through her back, but up and down her arm.

She turned to find the stranger's heavy blade half buried in Narcissus's forearm, the weapon trapped by the big Celt's bracer and bone while his blood flowed freely from the wound. "Narcissus!" she screamed, sharing his pain, her own racing heart threatening to over-whelm her. Without missing a beat, their attacker blinked back, letting go of the weapon to avoid a wild thrust from Vesper's gladius.

"I'll live," he grunted through clenched teeth, his eyes shooting open when the sword vanished from his wound to appear in the stranger's hand once more. "Stop him!"

Shifting her gaze from Narcissus to the bloodied weapon pointed at her once more, it was clear the stranger was there for her, and her alone. Her presence was a danger to the man she cared about, and if she wanted to keep him safe, she would have to fight this man somewhere else, some-where far away. Drawing on one of her first lessons, she opened herself to the weave, clutching a random thread vibrating in front of her. The alley, and everything in it, including the strange vanished, and Vesper jumped, the world little more than a blur as she rode the threads that bound reality together. A powerful wave crashed over her, and Vesper choked on a mouthful of bitter saltwater while fighting to stay afloat, deep ocean currents threatening to pull her down. Fighting for breath, Vesper reached for another thread, the world around her blurring once more until she found herself burying her feet in rich brown soil, overlooking a green vineyard that stretched as far as the eye could see, the vines heavy with plump grapes ready for the harvest, while the hint of the sun's yellow rays peeked over the crescent of the fading night sky.

Vesper sighed in relief and began to wipe water from her face and hair when the stranger appeared from nowhere, his brown tunic drip-ping with seawater. "You cannot run from me," he said. "There is no place I cannot find you!"

Vesper stepped back, cocking her head in confusion. "Why are you hunting me? I have done nothing wrong," she began, holding out a hand in front of her. "What accusations have been made against me?"

The stranger halted, lowering his blade a few inches. "The accused may know their crimes," he said, narrowing his eyes. "You have been accused of—"

"Not accusations," she pleaded, desperation in her voice. "Questions, I have so many questions. Who are you? Are there more like us? More chosen?"

"You have stolen from the Olodumare the almighty... using his Ase for your own selfish purposes."

Vesper shook her head, her nostrils flaring in anger at the accusation. "Never! How could I? I have never—"

"You bear the mark of your stolen power out in the open for all to see!" he said, pointing at her with his heavy blade.

"You mean these," she asked, following his gaze to the tattoos that stretched across her collarbone, the images that Eshu had used to mark her as one of his own. "No, Eshu placed these on me."

"You lie well," he snarled, taking a threatening step forward. "As all of your kind do."

"I'm not lying," she said, backing away. "They were given to me by Eshu; he told me it was his mark. That he would call on me for favors."

The geometric patterns on his arms took on a soft glow, flashing amber and gold in the dim morning light. Vesper's brow shot up when the tattoos on her arms did the same, pulsing in unison with his, casting them both in a waning light. After a moment, he hooked his rune-covered blade to his waist, frowning at her. "You're telling the truth, but it changes nothing. The Ase must be returned, and you must be punished."

"What's your name? Are you Ose?"

"I am Seye, a seeker of Ogun. Chosen of the Nok people," he said, puffing out his chest.

"I'm Vesper," she said, shuddering like she was about to laugh and cry at the same time. "I was told that I was the last of the chosen, the last of the Ose."

"More lies! The Ose abandoned their duty to the garden centuries ago, heading north in pursuit of some foolish conflict. I doubt any survived to this day," he said as the patterns on his arms pulsed faster. "As for the chosen, we are few in number, but still doing Olodumare work. Keeping the blight from overcoming the world."

"No... I am Ose. I swear!"

"It does not matter," he said, raising his arms over his head, his deep voice echoing over the vineyard as he began to sing in a language that sounded familiar and foreign at the same time. Vesper gasped, blinking in awe when he shouted a single word, and the patterns on his arms came to life, separating, from his physical form, dozens of small spheres, some the size of raindrops, others larger than a man's fist.

"What are you doing?" she asked as the spheres began to circle one another, spinning faster with every orbit.

"My duty is to return you to the garden, so that what you have stolen can be removed. Prepare yourself."

"I have done nothing wrong, committed no crime," said Vesper, taking a step back while shifting her gaze to see the weave, a shudder running through her as she drank in its power. "I will not let you take me."

Seye extended his arm, and the spinning spheres took on a life of their own, bolting toward her in fury of cascading light. "Judgment has been rendered; the choice is no longer yours," he finished with a shout.

Vesper reacted on instinct, weaving a gladius made of pure light, cleaving at the glowing orbs as they hissed toward her. She gritted her teeth through pain when an orb touched her blade and exploded in a torrent of sparks that stung her eyes and sizzled against her skin. "Stop this! I don't want to hurt you. We are kindred, part of the same distant tribe!" she began, her voice full of desperation.

"You fight like an untrained child," he said, stretching his arms toward her as another wave shot toward her, forcing Vesper on the defensive. "I doubt you could hurt me if you tried."

"I think you'll find that I'm full of surprises," she said, spinning her body and blade at an angle that redirected the bulk of the glowing orbs instead of shattering them. Sending them exploding behind her

"Simple tricks, tricks that won't save you," he said, once more drawing his hooked blade and stalking toward her, the glowing orbs out in front of him, leading the way.

Ignoring his comment, Vesper channeled all of the Ase she had drawn from the weave into her limbs making her feel stronger than a charging elephant and faster than a racing cheetah. Seya brought his heavy blade down in a titanic swing, and Vesper knocked it aside as if it were a child's toy, then taking a tactic from Narcissus, she kicked out with all her strength, her boot slamming into his chest with enough force that he took to the air, tearing through a canopy of grapevines and landing hard on his backside a dozen feet away. "I will not come with you," she said, charging to stand over him, in a single breath, her tone even and measured—calm. "I am free now, and I will never be leashed again. Not by you or anyone else. Understood?"

"I have a duty," he began, vanishing and reappearing a short hop away. "I will never stop hunting you." His face twisted into a mask of pain as he rose on shaking legs, spitting out gobs of bright-red blood while clutching at his chest.

"I understand duty," she said with a nod, casting a wary eye at him when he shouted a single word, and the spinning spheres reappeared and circled around him once more. "But sometimes it needs to be put aside for the greater good."

Seye pushed out his lower lip, frowning at her. "Not for me." The strange chosen unleashed a burning shower of glowing spheres that raced toward her. Vesper changed tactics, using her Ase-enhanced legs to vault over the volley at the last second, landing with the grace of a hunting cat, beside him. Without missing a beat, he drew his hooked blade and swung it at her in a single smooth motion, forcing her to bend backward to avoid losing her head.

Vesper twisted to get back her footing, only to find herself on her bottom, air blasting from her lungs after Seye swept her legs out from under her with the hook in his blade. In response, Vesper kicked out blindly, smiling when her foot connected to his face with a satisfying crunch, snapping his head back and sending him staggering out of her field of view. "Stop this," she shouted, vaulting to her feet, her eyes darting in all directions.

She caught sight of him not far away on a low rise, the rising sun blazing behind him while he twisted his arms in a complex pattern that made her belly clench with worry. Shifting her vision, she watched in grim fascination as he pulled hundreds of threads together, pulling them into a complex pattern she couldn't begin to understand. It was clear that he had far more experience than she did, and if she didn't stop him here and now, he would take her, and she would never see Narcissus again. Drawing deep on the Ase in her blood, Vesper did the one simple thing she knew well that might stop him. Straining with all her might, she clutched at the threads of Ase he was controlling, tearing the writhing threads from his grasp, gasping in ecstasy when a rush of power coursed through her veins, setting her senses on edge, her entire being vibrating like she was immersed in pure joy.

"What did you do!" he shouted, falling to his knees while clutching his head, the geometric patterns on his arms and shoulders fading to a dull gray against his dark skin.

Vesper shuddered, sucking in deep breaths while trying to control her racing heart and trembling hands. With a supreme effort, she walked slowly up the rise toward him, ripping away every thread of Ase he tried to grasp, denying him the power to harm her. She approached him with her gladius out in front of her, placing the glowing weapon under his chin, her meaning clear. "If you move, if you breathe in a way I don't like, my blade will pierce your throat, understood?"

"Yes," he rasped, through gritted teeth, while his dark skin glistened with sweat.

"I have no understanding of what conflict you have with me. Eshu's mark was given to me by the loa himself, a boon for my service to him. If you have a problem with that, you can summon him yourself and deal with the consequences of that action."

"Impossible. The primal loa, they no longer answer. The Ase could have only been stolen from—"

"I met him; he marked me," said Vesper, pressing the tip of her gladius against his throat, the odor of burnt flesh wafting to her nostrils. "And I'm tired of being called a liar and a thief. We Ose... are honorable people, bound by duty and loyalty, so keep those words from your tongue, or I will remove it." The word left Vesper's mouth, and she forced her features to stillness, amazed to hear the threat coming from her. The months spent around Narcissus were having an effect on her, in the strangest ways.

"How are you doing this?" he said, weakly trying and failing to grasp the threads of Ase that Vesper gripped tightly.

"Can't you?" she asked, raising an eyebrow.

Seye only shook his head, his eyes drilling into her. "To draw out another's power." These things are unknown to my people."

Vesper was taken aback, and for a moment she thought he was lying, but the wide-eyed look of terror on his face spoke volumes. Staring at the threads of power she was holding, she looked at him, noticing for the first time that she was not only channeling the power he took from the weave, but she was somehow controlling the Ase in the man's blood, the life force that was a part of him; she was killing him. "If I return your strength to you, will you stop this? Will you leave me be?" she asked, knowing the answer before he responded.

He gave her a hard look, his mouth twisting with anger until finally, he looked away. "No, never," he said at last, shaking his head.

"Most people would have lied," she said, her shoulders slumping in disappointment. "I see that we are not so different, duty bound, no matter the cost. You will never stop, so I will have to stop you."

"Do what you must."

Vesper cursed, pressing her lips together as she drew back her gladius, aiming for his throat. "Such a waste."

The blade was about to pierce his throat when suddenly he plunged his hands in the rich soil, vanishing in the blink of an eye before she could end his life. Vesper spun in place, expecting Seye to come at her from any direction, but when the moments ticked by, and nothing happened, she let out a breath she didn't know she was holding. Realizing he had fled. With a shudder she released the Ase she was holding, crumpling to the ground and shaking in exhaustion, her limbs weak from the effort of holding so much power for so long.

She sat for a long time watching the sun rise high in the morning sky, replaying every moment of the battle in her mind, dissecting every word said. "There are more chosen... more like me," she muttered to herself at last, her heart beating faster with a strange mix of excitement and fear. She was no longer alone. Someone could teach her; she just had to find them and convince them not to kill her.

FOUR
THE SENATOR AND THE MATRON

"Lady Lucilla!" said Senator Adventus, his smile widening as he took her hands in his. "They told me you had been banished. There have even been rumors that your brother sent a legionnaire to kill you!"

Lucilla squeezed his hands back in a tight grip before letting go, relieved that the senator was happy to see her. "Rumors of my demise have been greatly exaggerated," she said. "However, they serve my plans, so I am content to let them stand."

The portly senator ran a hand through his shock of thick, white hair, bobbing his head in agreement. "I understand. A wise choice given the recent slave rebellion and your brother's current state of madness," he said, his eyes darting to her companion, who wore a woolen hood to protect her braided hair from the winter rains. "But let's not just stand here like strangers; come in and dry off. I was breaking my fast in the garden. Come, I have a new vintage I want you to try."

"Your estates are impressive; you have an eye for beauty," she said, following at the senator's side while he guided them through the wide halls of his country estate, stopping every now and again to eye the finery on display. Priceless paintings and tapestries from every corner of the empire lined their path, while blades and axes, weapons of all kinds were on display in cases of rare wood and glass, the senator having been a general, and then governor, in Arabia for many decades.

"The rewards of a life spent in the saddle, protecting the thing I love most in the world," he said, puffing out his chest with pride. "Rome."

"I'm sure your wife would raise an objection to such words," she said, drinking in a deep breath, a sense of calm rolling over her as they stepped out into a terrasse where a vine-covered pagoda provided shade from the relentless winter drizzle that hadn't slowed in days. One of his many servants led them to a small table that overlooked his vast estate, with green rolling hills of grapes to the east, and an orchard filled with olive trees to the west.

"Oh, she knew how I was when we married. I'm sure it came as no surprise to her," he said with a laugh, settling in on a padded bench. "Now, you must tell me who is your exotic companion, and what you would have from me," he said.

Lucilla settled in across from him, smiling as a slave poured her a cup of wine from a pitcher that beaded with condensation and the promise of cool wine, the girl doing the same for her companion before scurrying off to wait for the senator's beck and call. "This is Mother Ayaba, and we have come to make an indecent proposal, Senator."

Senator Adventus sat up straight at the use of his formal title, tilting his head in curiosity as he poured a bit of sapa into his wine to sweeten it. "I'm flattered," he said, smiling at the pair of them. "But I am far too old for such things!"

"This is no time for jokes," said Mother Ayaba, her kind smile vanishing behind a hard-eyed gaze. "The world is in danger, and while we laugh and joke, Commodus plans to burn it to the ground. He must be stopped... no matter the cost."

"Are you mad, woman?" he said, coughing into his cup. "Senator Magnus barely escaped with his life, and now half the men of the senate have done as I have, retreating to their country estates and waiting for things to settle down."

"Now is not the time to hide," said Lucilla, placing a restraining hand on the old matron's, leaning forward and speaking in low tones. "My brother will not relent in his plans just because you are out of sight. He grows worse with each passing day. He means to eliminate the senate. We must stand against him, no matter the cost."

"You exaggerate, my dear. He cannot do such a thing," said the senator. "And in truth, I have no desire to challenge him and end up crucified in the arena for all of Rome to see."

"But Senator —" she began, locking eyes with him.

"No, Lucilla," he said, looking down at his hands, his face reddening. "I am an old man. I have fought my battles and won my wars. I no longer have the luxury of youth on my side for foolish pursuits as you do."

Lucilla frowned, looking down on him with pity while remembering him as a younger man, a man who was strong and bold, a man who defied and defeated Rome's enemies. "If I were a lesser woman, I would pity you, but because of who you are, I shall try to remember you as the titan you once were."

"That's unkind, young lady—"

She jumped in her skin when Mother Ayaba slapped the palms of her hands against the stone table, glaring at the senator. "Enough of this cowardice," she said in a powerful voice. "My patience for you Romans is at an end. I will endure this no more."

Before either of them could respond, the older woman, with the kind face, spoke a word so vile that Lucilla's stomach turned with nausea. Lucilla paled when she found herself frozen in place, her body no longer in control.

"What is the meaning of this?" said Senator Adventus, his eyes widening with panic as she took a step toward him, drawing a bone dagger with a leather-wrapped hilt, from under the stola that covered her shoulders and fell past her waist.

"This is not as we discussed," began Lucilla, finding that she could speak but not move, her eyes never leaving the bone-white blade. "We are to... convince... not kill. Have you gone mad?"

Mother Ayaba ignored her, spinning the bone blade in her fingers while cutting shallow, almost invisible, gashes on the senator's arms, leaving thin lines of bright crimson on his pale flesh. "Come, Sandawei," she muttered in low tones, pressing herself against him, whispering into his ear. "Come, quick!" The old matron continued chanting in a strange tongue that set Lucilla's teeth on edge, while at the same time digging the tip of her blade into the senator's soft belly.

Senator Adventus stood stock still, unmoving, his lips trembling while his face reddened in anger. "If you mean to kill me, do it quickly," he began in a voice shaking with rage. "Because if I live, there is no place you will be able to hide from my wrath."

"You have a strong will," said Mother Ayaba. "Few are able to speak through this weave, much less find the strength to offer empty threats." With a final chant, the blade flashed a bright white, and she plunged the blade into his belly, a shadow falling over the garden as if the sun had vanished to an eclipse.

Whatever Mother Ayaba did to hold her in place vanished, and she managed a step toward them, almost falling to the ground, while beads of sweat rolled down her brow. "You monster," Lucilla stammered.

"No monster," said the matron in a thin, reedy voice, pulling the blade from his stomach in a shaking hand. Lucilla gasped in shock when the weapon came away bloodless, the white bone blade unstained. "Just a person willing to do what is necessary."

The senator's eyes flashed from cobalt to crimson, shifting from one color to another with every heartbeat, until finally, he blinked and they became a milky white that covered not only the iris, but the entire pupil. "What have you done to me," he said, drawing in a shuddering breath, running his hands over his belly.

"I have returned to you the fires of youth," she said, the bone dagger vanishing under her shawl just as quickly as it had appeared.

Senator Adventus spun in place, his laugh booming across the rolling hills. "I feel like I could fight ten men."

"What did you do to him?" asked Lucilla, catching herself on the table, able to move again.

"I have given him a gift, the strength to fight with us if he so desires," she said in a cracking voice, the kindly smile returning to her face.

"I will," said the senator before Lucilla could say another word. "I, and everything I have is at your service. Together we shall remove this tyrant and return Rome to its former glory. Greater glories!"

Mother Ayaba pulled her woolen hood over her head, her shoulders rolling in on themselves, leaving her looking old and frail. "Good, then I will call on you when the time is right," she said, turning to face Lucilla, and speaking in a voice that cracked with each word. "Come, Augusta, we have many more senators to visit if we are to put you in your rightful place as ruler of this great empire."

Senator Adventus gave her an approving nod while he spun in place, laughing like a child. Watching the old woman vanish into the house, she replayed the events in her mind, her belly churning with fear at what madness she had gotten herself into.

FIVE

POWER AND GRACE

Narcissus raised his head to the dark sky, breathing in a lungful of cool air before ducking through the entrance of the crumbling insulae, following Isi and Lillith up the gloom-filled stairwell. "What kind of rat-infested hovel is this? It looks like it's about to fall over," he growled, wiping away the rainwater dripping from his short beard while climbing the crumbling stairs two at a time, every muscle tense while he looked everywhere at once.

"The choice is not mine," squeaked Isi, over his shoulder. "This is where my contact told me to meet."

"I'm starting to regret my decision to not simply sell you," said Lillith from up ahead of them. "I grow tired of these dead ends and angry contacts who only speak to you because you owe them denarii."

"If anyone will know where the emperor's sister had been spirited to... it will be this man. I swear!"

Narcissus crowded in at the top of the landing with Lillith and Isi, gagging from the smell of the old sailor's salt-stained coat that stank of mildew and sour sweat. "I wish to find Lady Lucilla, but I fear for Vesper," he said, reaching out through their bond, a smile coming to her face when he felt that she was sleeping on comfortable sheets. The sensation from their connection made it feel as if he were there at her side, drinking in her smell, her warmth.

"She can handle herself... far better than the rest of us," said Lillith, fighting with an oil lamp until the flame caught, pushing back the gloom and casting them all in a pale amber glow. "Which apartment, Isi?"

"This way, down near the end," he said, bopping his head and then leading them down the dingy corridor past several apartments, until stopping in front of a flimsy wooden door that looked like all the others. "This should be it."

"I know she can take care of herself," began Narcissus, pushing him aside while he ran his palm up and down the door that barred their path, worried that if he pushed his shoulder against it with any kind of force, the entire building might come down on his head. "But after her battle with that strange attacker, she was exhausted... and now we have left her alone to follow this idiot on a fool's errand."

"Don't worry," said Lillith. "The senator's country house is far from any major roads; I doubt anyone would find her... that's the reason we chose it?"

When Vesper had vanished with the stranger, Narcissus had feared the worst, but by the grace of the gods, she had returned to him not long after, exhausted yet exuberant.

Asking for time. They had returned to the country home that served as their base of operations since they had stolen their freedom, while he and Lucilla continued the search for Lucilla, so far with little to show for it. "Step back," said Narcissus, putting his shoulder to the door, splintering the ancient wood with little effort. Pushing his way through the rotted wood, he entered a graffiti-covered room filled with broken furnishings and garbage piled high in the corners. Empty except for a few rats that sniffed at him before returning to poking through the filth in the room. Spinning on his heels, he glared at Isi until he looked away, the sailor's face reddening in shame. "He leads us in circles," said Narcissus. "We've been to every filthy popinae in Rome—and now this!"

"He told me he'd be here," said Isi, speaking quickly. "I've never met him, but Azrael is one of the few Frumentarii that Commodus did not dismiss."

"Azrael," said Lillith, immediately drawing her gladius and shield, her eyes darting in all directions. "I know of him. He is a dangerous man, an assassin that has served the empire for longer than most."

"You want us to trust a man still serving Commodus?" asked Narcissus with a frown, towering over the stinking sailor.

"There is a reason Commodus could not get rid of him. It is said that only the dead know his face," said Lillith. "We must go! Go now!"

Narcissus flinched, throwing Isi an angry look before continuing. "I will break every bone in your stinking body for this."

"I didn't betray you; I swear!" he said, raising his hands defensively as Narcissus took a step closer to him. "He told me he knows where she is, that he would lead us to her."

"You're a bigger fool than I thought," said Narcissus, reaching for his throat, halting when Isi glanced at something behind them, his eyes shooting open and his weathered face paling. Without thinking, Narcissus spun to his right, putting his back to the wall just in time to avoid the dart that buried itself deep into Isi's chest, a hollow rattle escaping his throat as his body crumpled to the floor. Adrenaline pumped through Narcissus's, every muscle tense as he scanned the gloom for the source of attack. He caught the glint of steel and dove to his right just as a black-clad man, with his face hidden, erupted from the shadows, his oversized cloak billowing like it was caught in the wind, concealing his movements as his blade flashed toward Narcissus's heart.

"Azrael!" shouted Lillith, stepping in front of Narcissus, her shield blocking his gladius just before it pierced his chest, the clash of steel deafening in the small room. "What is the meaning of this!?"

"Tying up loose ends," he said, glancing at Isi's fallen form, "and collecting on a profitable bounty." The assassin danced back, concealing the naked steel of his gladius in his billowing cloak for a heartbeat, before he came at her again, the weapon flashing at Lillith from every direction, driving her back on her heels while she alternated with her sword and shield to block his furious attacks.

"The only loose thread cut today will be your life," said Lillith, ducking behind her shield while charging at the assassin, catching only air and shredding bits of the billowing cloak as she raced past him.

"I expected more from the great Lillith," he mocked, flowing around her to strike at her back. "You're slow... so weak!"

Lillith somehow blocked his swing with a desperate reach over her shoulder with her gladius. A heartbeat later, she spun in place, clipping him with her shield, sending him reeling back. "Fast enough for you... and that's all that matters."

Seeing that Lillith had his attention, Narcissus pushed himself away from the wall with a roar, taking advantage of his long reach to grab at the assassin's loose clothing, catching only air as he spun away from Lillith, to focus on Narcissus, his blade flicking out like a serpent's tongue, stabbing with such speed and skill that he left jagged scars on the big Celt's leather vest and steel bracers. Narcissus raised his arms in an X to block a vicious blow when Azrael feinted, twisting his body to catch Narcissus in the belly with a heavy boot, quickly followed by an elbow to the center of his chest that doubled him over, blasting the air from his lungs. The assassin moved to finish him when Lillith slammed into his back with her shield, driving him toward the wall. Instead of resisting, he used their combined momentum to run up the wall, flipping back and landing behind the former djambe. Lillith started to turn, but he was faster, his blade cutting low and slicing into her hamstring, sending her crumpling to the floor with a screech of agony.

"All too easy," he said, drawing back his gladius for the killing blow. Just as the blade was about to pierce her back, Narcissus threw himself between them, catching the thrust on his flank, the razor-sharp gladius ripping through leather and flesh with ease. Azrael's eyes shot open in surprise as they stumbled along, the pair of them falling into a heap of twisting bodies and blood.

"I don't think so," said Narcissus, locking the other man's forearm in an iron grip, then before he could recover slamming a meaty fist into the bridge of Azrael's nose when he tried to pull out his blade, sending his eyes rolling back in his head.

"Narcissus? Are you still alive?" shouted Lillith in a strained voice. "Or are you just taking your time with Azrael? They say you always enjoyed killing slowly."

"I am here," grunted Narcissus, his breath catching in his throat when he shifted his weight to roll on his back. "But I should be dead for my foolishness."

"Is Azrael dead?"

Narcissus sat up, pressing his hands tight against the wound while the room spun. "He lives, but I may just kill him out of spite for putting this blade in my side."

"Don't pull it out!"

Narcissus rolled his eyes, standing to his full height on shaking legs, slamming a heavy boot into Azrael's belly for good measure. "Of course not, woman!" he growled. "You think this the first time I've had a blade in my gut? I'll live, although I will need a trip to the medicus." He walked over to where Lillith lay in a pool of her own blood, her normally beautiful face twisted in a mask of agony.

"He's dead," she said, pointing at Isi's fallen form with her chin. Cursing, she put her back to the wall while tearing away bits of her stola to make a bandage, deftly tying the material around her bleeding thigh.

"No great loss," he said, frowning at the fallen sailor. "Although... our path to find Lucilla has once again ground to a halt."

Lillith shook her head, a wry smile coming to her face. "Isi was always a fool, but there was wisdom in hunting down Azrael. There probably isn't much that goes on in the empire that he doesn't know. We just have to find a way to make him talk."

Narcissus glanced down once more to the blade in his flank, a feral grin coming to his face. "I will make him talk."

"Good, he has a lot to pay for," said Lillith. "Help me up, so we can get out of here. Azrael usually works alone, but it's best if we don't take any chances."

He sneered at her outstretched hand, shaking his head. "You have another leg, use it."

"You would save my life and then leave me to die in my own blood?" she said, gritting her teeth while using the wall to push herself up. "And yet my daughter thinks you're noble, so honorable."

A low chuckle escaped his throat as he limped back to the fallen assassin, ripping away parts of his dark cloak to start binding his arms and legs. "I am. Just not with the likes of you! After that day in the house of Bacchus, I swore I would never let you touch me again, and I intend to keep my oath."

"I did what I did to survive," snarled Lillith, glaring at him. "Not that a simple-minded barbarian like you would understand."

"Simple minded enough not to care what you think of me." Lifting the assassin, he slammed his fist to his face once more for good measure, nodding in satisfaction when his head rolled back and forth. "But having enough wisdom never to trust a treacherous snake like you ever again."

"Very well, I'll do it myself," said Lillith, dragging herself to Isi's corpse, unbuckling the fallen sailor's scabbard and sword and placing the tip on the floor, her face an unreadable mask as she adjusted her weight to walk with the makeshift cane. "I always have, and it seems I always will."

Ignoring her, Narcissus bound Azrael's arms in strips of his own cloak, then did his best to wrap the wound on his flank. The assassin groaned when Narcissus bent him backward to bind his legs and arms together, and in a moment of curiosity, he pulled down his mask, Narcissus choking on his tongue when he saw a familiar face. "By the gods, I know this man."

"Who is he?" asked Lillith, limping to his side and staring at Azrael with a blank look on her face.

"Jacob," he grumbled, shaking his head in confusion. "He's the medicus at Ludus Magnus—or at least he was before the revolt. I've known him for years. He saved Vesper's life."

Lilith's brow shot up, and a smile creased her face. "A Jewish slave posing as a medicus is, in truth, one of the greatest assassins to have ever wielded a blade. Impressive."

"We should get back to Vesper. Maybe she might be able to convince him to help us; he was always kind to her."

"For once we agree. Let us pray that he has the answers we seek, and that for Lucilla's sake, she lives long enough for us to find her."

SIX
PATHS

Lucilla paced the opulent room in a fury, cursing her stupidity. In her desperation to be free of Commodus and his madness, she had traded one tyrant for another, traded one cage for another. After months living in squalor, she was once more surrounded with everything worthy of her station, but it was just a prettier cage than the one beneath the Colosseum. Gilded mirrors reflected her beauty at every turn, while colorful dresses and stolas dyed in the rarest of colors filled the wardrobe. The massive bed she slept in, the fine chairs she sat upon, even the cushions scattered around the room were covered in fine silk that must have cost a Caesar's ransom. Each day she dined on fine foods prepared to perfection, washing it all down with rare vintages of wine that dazzled her tongue, all available at the ring of a tiny brass bell near the door, instantly summoning a dozen slaves, who would rush to do whatever she wished, but she could not come and go as she pleased. Leaving her room only when Mother Ayaba summoned her.

The time she had spent with the old woman had terrified her, and Lucilla woke most nights in a cold sweat, the words of the matron's ritual still ringing in her ears while she clutched at her chest, searching for the bloodless wound that the Sandawei woman had left in the hearts of every senator they had visited together. What worried her the most was the reaction of Rome's most powerful men. After the matron's ritual, each man had pledged their loyalty to the matron, joyful for the power and youth she had granted them, never questioning the how or why.

Drawing in a deep breath to calm her mind, Lucilla glided over to the open window, gazing out over the empty garden, wondering for the thousandth time where she was. The flora was typical of a country villa, where most Roman patricians lived when they were not city bound. Decorated with roses, oleanders, lilies, and amaranth, while other parts served to grow the more common vegetables that were part of the Roman diet: beans, olives, and peas, but Lucilla never saw a single soul working. In fact, it was clear that the garden was the domain of Mother Ayaba, with even Kubwa, the man with the red mask, entering only when summoned. Beyond the garden was only wilderness, with not even a road in sight, much less the travelers. The longer she stayed, the more she regretted her decision to work with the Sandawei matron. Her desperation for freedom, her desire to remove her brother from power had thrown her into an impossible situation, and now with the perspective of time, she decided that escape was her only option.

Steeling her nerve, she rang the brass bell, her pulse quickening when she hefted a clay lamp near the door... and waited. A few moments later, the young man who served as her valet opened the door with a pleasant smile plastered across his face. Terrified of losing her will to do what she had to, Lucilla closed her eyes and swung with all her might, a screech escaping her lips when the lamp struck something hard, the clay shattering in her hands as her heart beat out of her chest. "Apologies," she whispered to the fallen valet when she opened her eyes at last. Fighting her first impulse to help him, she instead knelt at his side, prying a brass key from his hand and then sneaking into the empty hall, her eyes darting in all directions.

Lucilla found herself walking down a colonnade with closed

doors to her right while overlooking the main atrium to her left. The large room was usually where guests entered, and it was decorated to impress. A large skylight provided light that dazzled off the blue and gold mosaic tiles and brightly colored statues of well-muscled men, while a series of wide benches surrounded a large reflecting pool filled with crystal-clear rainwater. Tearing her eyes away from the beautiful entryway, she rushed past the marble columns, hunting for stairs that would take her down, or an open door that would lead to—

"Lady Lucilla, what are you doing out of your rooms?"

Lucilla's eyes snapped open in fear, and for a heartbeat, her mind raced to find a lie as to why she was out of her rooms, but then she remembered who she was and the role she'd assumed for her entire life. Drawing in a deep breath through her nose, she turned slowly, raising a fine eyebrow at the female slave gliding toward her. "This is totally unacceptable," said Lucilla, pushing out her chin while glaring at the girl.

The girl slid to a halt, her liquid-brown eyes widening with shock. "Apologies Domina," she said automatically. "What—"

"I should have all of you whipped!" she interrupted, looking the girl up and down with an appraising glance. She was young, with the caramel-colored skin, dark hair, and round features found in slaves from the east, Anatolia or Syria**, and** having the timid look of someone who had been a slave since childhood.

"Domina, please," she began, prostrating herself while spreading her arms wide. "What have we done to offend you?"

"One of you filthy slaves came to my room. Drunk!" said Lucilla. "Pawing at me like an animal! I was forced to punish him myself."

The slave pressed her lips together, shaking her head in confusion before continuing, "That should never have been permitted. I will speak to Mother—"

"You will do no such thing," said Lucilla. "This is beyond your station. I will speak to the matron myself. Where is she?"

"Lady Lucilla—"

Lucilla stepped forward, towering over the girl. "Augusta!"

"Apologies, Augusta," she said, raising her hands above her head protectively, "But—"

"I can tell the matron you were part of this foolishness, or I can forget you interrupted me. Which do you prefer?"

The girl's lips quivered, and she looked away, her hands tying in knots. "Please, Domina, I want no part of this."

"Good! Now go on with your task, and I will try to forget you interrupted me!"

"Gratitude, you are a beacon of kindness, Domina."

Lucilla dismissed the slave girl with a nod, and she squealed away, casting desperate looks over her shoulder before vanishing around a corner. Letting out a breath she didn't know she was holding, Lucilla continued along the colonnade until she found a narrow set of stairs meant for servants or slaves, a sense of relief flooding through her as she emerged from the dimly lit staircase to find herself in a small kitchen, her mouth watering when the smell of roasted pork filled her nostrils. Gratefully, the room was empty, and the noblewoman dashed from room to room until she caught a glimpse of the reflecting pool and atrium she had spied from above.

Lucilla fought the urge to run when she saw the pair of carved wooden doors inlaid with brass. Instead, she walked slowly as if she belonged. She found it strange that even here, aside from a small shrine with a few flickering candles meant to honor Lares, god of the hearth, not a soul was present.

Squaring her shoulders, she walked to the doors and pulled on the brass handles, cursing in frustration, but not surprised to find them shut tight. Fingering the brass lock, she fished out the key from the slave she had knocked out, turning and twisting it into the mechanism with little success. Lucilla stepped back, closing her eyes and breathing deeply to calm her mind. She and Tiberius had a country villa on the cliffs that overlooked the Bay of Naples, a vast sprawling place with a full staff of slaves and servants that catered to their every whim, including waiting at the entrance so that visitors received the proper greetings when they arrived. This place was empty by comparison, with the few slaves she had seen forced to take on multiple roles. It would only make sense to lock the doors, and that the slave closest to the entrance would greet visitors... and a key would be kept close.

"The shrine," whispered Lucilla, her composure forgotten as she raced to the small alcove, hunting for any sign of the key among the guttering candles and wax bust of some ancient ancestor. She covered her mouth to stifle a shriek when her fingers brushed against the smooth brass hidden behind a small statue, a smile coming to her face when she darted to the door, and the key slid in with little effort, and the door swung open to reveal a small gravel path which led through a high shrub in the distance.

She took a step out the door and jumped out of her skin when a voice called out from behind her: "I wouldn't step out there if I were you."

Lucilla recognized the hollow cadence even before she turned in place, unsurprised to find the Sandawei in the red mask stalking toward her. "Why? What does it matter to you?" she said.

"That way lies only death," he said, stopping an arm's length from her, his eyes full of amusement behind the garish skull that served to hide his face. "It matters to me that you keep your word. It matters to the senators who have pledged themselves to your banner, but most of all it matters to Mother Ayaba."

Lucilla's head swung back and forth between the sumptuous country house and the path. "No, I'm a slave here, trapped."

"Slave," he scoffed through the mask. "No, you are safe here, with every luxury worthy of your station. Why would you leave, especially when we are so close to elevating you to empress."

She looked past him and shook her head. The villa was filled with everything her heart could desire, every luxury she had wished for; the riches that had blinded her until now. "All of my life it has been the same," she said, staring at the path. "Pretty rooms with pretty dresses hanging in the wardrobe. All while my fate is controlled by someone else. My father, my husband, Then my brother… and now, Mother Ayaba."

"You make no sense," he said, stepping closer, reaching out. "When you are empress, you will have more power than you could desire. More than any Caesar in history. The men of the Senate will bow to your will; the people—"

"No!" she shouted. "They will bow to Mother Ayaba. Just as I will if I stay on this path."

Never breaking her gaze, he stepped aside, motioning that she return inside. "Come now, don't be a fool. Not now, when we are so close."

"You show your hand," said Lucilla with a smile. "You and Mother Ayaba need me far more than I need you. You need the men of the Senate to open their doors when you come calling. She needs them to trust her long enough for the ritual."

"To all of our benefit," he said, spreading his arms wide. "Now, come back inside, or I will make you!"

Gazing down the path that led to the unknown, she took a step back. It was clear to her that even if they made her Augusta, nothing would change… except for the size of her gilded cage. The unknown path would be a life without the comforts she had grown accustomed to, maybe even to her death, but it would be a life that was hers. "No!" The Man in the mask lunged for her, and Lucilla bolted, the world around her a shifting blur as she pumped her legs as fast as they would go.

"Don't go beyond the hedge," screamed a high-pitched voice from somewhere behind her. Worried that he was closing in, Lucilla pushed herself harder, her heart racing faster in an adrenaline-fueled mix of fear and exhilaration.

Reaching the hedge, she ignored his warning and blasted beyond the green wall of shrubbery, stumbling, staggering almost falling when instead of finding herself racing up and down the green rolling fields that she had seen from her window, the gravel path gave way to a dull, gray cobblestone path that stretched off into the gloom.

"Where am I?" she whispered, a chill running through her when the keen wailing of distant screams reached her ear.

"Did you think this was some simple country villa?" began the masked Sandawei, his chest heaving as he emerged from the tall, green hedge. "Did you think you could just walk out the door and return to your life?"

"This is how you took me from the prison, the place between," she said, her eyes falling on the ash-colored earth, just beyond the cobblestone path.

"Yes," he said, the skull covering his face looking far more terrifying when reflected in the dim light. "And as you can see, you have nowhere to go without me, without us!"

Lucilla grit her teeth together, her nostrils flaring as she glared at him. "I would give you a painful death if I could," she said, raising her chin. "You deserve no less—"

"Enough talk. The game is done!" he said, followed by a shout of power she knew well, a word Mother Ayaba used with every senator they had met. Lucilla gasped when a jolt coursed through her, her limbs going stiff, the air blasting out of her lungs as she fell hard, twisting at the last moment to land on her side instead of her face.

"Poor Lucilla," mocked the masked Sandawei, appearing above her as she gasped for breath. "We had so much hope for you, that you would be part of our great crusade. But if you cannot do this of your own free will, then we will have to force you." Without another word, he straddled her, sitting on her chest, showing her a bleached bone dagger with a leather-wrapped hilt. The hair on her arms stood on end when he shouted a single vile word, a word that began the ritual she had witnessed dozens of times. With deft hands, he carved shallow cuts on her skin, drawing jagged, square symbols up and down her arms and upper chest, his masterful cuts leaving a trail of blood dripping down her pale flesh while he chanted in his strange, halting tongue, the sky above him flashing a bright white as jagged bolts of lightning fell in the distance.

He drew the final rune on her shoulders, calling on ancient

power as he raised the dagger above his head. Lucilla had witnessed the ritual often enough to know what to expect and when he was vulnerable. The moment the blade flashed with a pale light, the force binding her vanished, and she made her move. With all her might, she punched him in the groin with one hand while slamming him under his chin with the other. He fell forward, and Lucilla wasted no time, twisting her hips to throw him off her.

"Fool woman, you'll pay for that!" he shouted in a voice she knew well.

Lucilla rolled to her feet, ignoring the pain in her arms and shoulders as she turned to face him, an icy chill running through her when she saw that his mask had fallen away, revealing a familiar face. "By the gods... Magnus! How?"

The weak-chinned senator sneered at her, his gaze falling on the discarded mask. "Do you think this matters?" he said, touching his face. "You won't remember any of this once I'm done with you."

"No, I have one final play," she whispered, a wide smile creasing her face as she stepped off the path, a piercing cold running through her body, threatening to shatter her bones.

"No!" he screeched behind her. "If you leave the path, you'll be lost forever among the damned."

"Then I will be damned!" she spat back at him, straightening her spine as she put one foot in front of the other, unflinching while lightning flashed overhead and thunder echoed in the distance, his voice fading the farther she drifted from the path, the screams of the damned growing louder with each step, calling her name over and over. She never faltered. Her chin raised high as she strode to eternal damnation.

SEVEN

MASKS

"The greatest assassin in the empire, masquerading as a common medicus. It's almost impossible to believe."

"Good enough to fool the great Lillith," spat Jacob.

Vesper's jaw fell open, seeing the rail-thin man in a new light as he fought against the thick rope binding him to the chair. "But... you were always so kind... and you saved my life," she said, wrapping her arms around herself. When her mother and Narcissus had brought the unconscious medicus to Senator Sabinus's villa, she was sure it was to help the man, but when they dragged him to the storage room and bound him, she frowned in confusion, only understanding when the former medicus woke.

Jacob bowed his head, his anger vanishing when their eyes met. "Yours was a life worth saving, my dear," he said, the easy smile she knew, returning to his face. "But these Romans, for what they did to my family, to my people. They all deserve the death I have delivered to them."

Narcissus crossed his arms over his massive chest, grinning with amusement. "Azrael, I know this name from your Hebrew texts. You hardly look like the angel of death, Jacob."

"Why, because I'm a skinny Jew?" he snapped, struggling against the coarse rope binding him to the chair. "Or because I fooled you, for years."

"Both, I guess," said the big Celt, with a shrug. "But you never had the look of a cold-blooded killer."

Jacob threw back his head, and a shrill laughter filled the small storage room. "Then I succeeded in my intent."

"Why the charade? Why not—"

"None of that matters," said Lillith, leaning in close to the assassin. "You live only for the information you can provide, so tell me, where is Lucilla?"

Jacob raised an eyebrow. "The emperor's sister? The only thing I know about her is that I should have killed her when I had the chance," he said, raising his chin. "That day in the infirmary when Vesper was injured, she was so close; it would have been easy. A quick twist of my blade, and another worthless Roman would have fallen to me. Why would I help you find her? She's just as bad as her wretched brother."

"You will tell me what I need to know," seethed Lillith, pulling back her arm to strike him.

"No," said Vesper in soft voice, catching her mother's arm before the blow could land. "I owe this man my life, and I told you, I will not do things your way. I will not make your mistakes."

Lillith glared at her with open rage, fighting against Vesper's grip. "He would have killed us today, Daughter. Look at my leg, at the wound on your Celt."

"Stand down, Mother."

Her mother flinched as if she'd been struck, before bowing her head in subjugation. "Your soft heart will cost you your life one day, or worse, the life of someone you love."

"On that day. I will mourn for the loss," she said, pushing her mother's hand away, "but until that day, I will be better than you ever were."

Jacob cocked his head, a half smile crossing his face as he

watched the exchange, "It was not personal, I only wished to collect the denarii. Only a fool would pass on such a lucrative bounty."

"Then I'll make you a simple offer," said Vesper, "Forget all about us, and we won't tell the empire who you really are. I'm sure the Frumentarii would love to know that their best assassin is a Jew, more so that he takes pleasure in killing Romans."

"You would only hasten my death...and you're not that kind of person," he said, smiling at her. "I can see it in your eyes."

Vesper pressed her lips together, her eyes meeting his as she looked for a way to reach him, "Jacob please. Lucilla is not like her brother. She has done everything in her power to help us overthrow him, and now she has paid the price."

"She got what she deserved for her conniving Roman ways," he spat.

She came closer to him, laying a hand on his shoulder, "You know that's not true Jacob, not every Roman is a monster. Lucilla is a good person...help us. If not out of doing the right thing, do it for me."

"You're wasting your time," said Lillith.

At her side Narcissus grunted in agreement, while waves of irritation flowing through their bond. "For once I agree with Lillith, nothing good can come from him. If you won't kill him, at least lock him up so he causes no further trouble."

Vesper cocked her head, thinking the same thing, "We've wasted enough time here. We'll ask Senator Sabinus if there is a cell that we—

"Wait!" interrupted Jacob, speaking quickly, "I will tell you what I know, if you are willing to do something for me."

"Now he wants to talk," laughed Narcissus.

"Tell me what you know. We'll consider if your information is worth our time," said Vesper.

The thin man frowned at her before finally nodding, "The last time I saw her, she was chained to the wall in the emperor's box, during the games."

"That is nothing new," said Narcissus. "We all saw her that day."

Vesper brushed his forearm with the tip of her fingers, calming him, "Please, after we fled. We need to know what happened to her."

"I don't know what happened after, I fled like everyone else," he said, "but I overheard her talking to the emperor's courtesan, Marcia."

"And?" asked Lillith.

Jacob ignored them, his eyes never leaving Vesper's. "Commodus told her that his sister would be his prisoner forever trapped in the hypogeum, forgotten by the world."

"The hypogeum?" asked Vesper.

"The underbelly of the Colosseum," said Narcissus, his pale skin flushing a deep shade of red as anger flowed through their bond.

"Is she still alive?" asked Vesper, leaning in close to the assassin, close enough that she could smell some sort of mint on his breath.

"I don't know," said Jacob, looking away with a shrug. "The conditions down there are brutal, and most slaves don't last long in that heat."

Vesper leaned back, looking back and forth between Narcissus and her mother, "We have to go to her—"

"Vesper, It's been six months, I doubt she still lives," said Narcissus, resting a heavy hand on her shoulder.

"We have to try, we have to look!" began Vesper, meeting each of their eyes in turn, daring them to say differently, "If it was me...Lucilla would try." she finished in a low voice.

Narcissus wrapped her in his arms and her heart quickened as she drank in his scent, his warmth. "Then we will try," he said, his voice rumbling in her ear.

Vesper smiled into his chest, wanting more, wanting to be with him. Instead, with a sigh she pushed him away and turned to their captive, "Name your price Jacob, what would you have of me?"

A tight-lipped smile stretched across the former medicus's face and the ropes binding him to the chair fell away as he stood to his full height. "Excellent," he said, rubbing his wrists.

"Snake!" said Lillith, hobbling back on her good leg while unsheathing the gladius and pointing it at him.

"Enough, Mother! If he had planned to hurt us, he would have."

Jacob's smile widened, showing his long white teeth. "You are correct, my dear. I swear by Almighty God that once I realized that it was you in charge, I had no intention of doing any harm."

"Then why the charade?" asked Narcissus.

He shrugged, shaking away the rest of the rope. "Apologies. It is difficult to undo a lifetime of caution and deception. In any case, our goals are in alignment, you only need to provide distraction, and our bargain will be complete."

"And what would that be," said Lillith, returning her weapon to its sheath, her eyes never blinking. "How in your crazed mind do our goals align?"

"In two days, every slave that attempted escape, along with those recaptured will be executed ad gladium."

A chill ran down Vesper's spine, her mind racing back to her first days in Rome. She had faced the same justice, sentenced to die at the hand of Rome's gladiators. She had survived, but the memory still haunted her, and she often woke from nightmares of the moment, soaked to the skin with her heart pounding out of her chest of being back on the sands, watching her father die, before finally facing off against the bronzed warriors herself. "How many?" she asked, swallowing hard.

"Thousands." said the assassin in a flat tone, his voice empty and without emotion.

Lillith scoffed, "We cannot save thousands of slaves who were foolish enough to be caught again."

"Mother?" said Vesper, frowning at her.

"We do not need to save thousands, only one," said Jacob.

"Who?" asked Vesper.

"My older brother."

Narcissus frowned at him, crossing his arms over his thick chest, "I still don't see how our goals align."

"When Emperor Hadrian ordered the Jews from Rome, I was just a child. Those that did not leave soon enough were enslaved. They came for my entire family in the middle of the night. I never saw my father or mother again, and I can hardly remember the faces of my sisters. But the Almighty God performed a miracle, and I was sold alongside my brother, Linus."

"Linus was, is, your brother?" asked Vesper, gawking at him.

Narcissus sucked in a sharp breath, and a shock of wild emotion passed through their bond. "Impossible," he snarled. "He escaped with us, and left here weeks ago, heading for Neapolis.

"Yes," said Jacob, nodding to her. "Linus looked more like a Roman than a Jew, and against my wishes, he hid his faith, spending his life posing as a gladiator while we plotted and planned our revenge."

"So, what do you need us for?" asked Lillith.

Jacob locked his arms behind his back, his face a mask of stone. "Well, the three of you are the most wanted people in Rome. Your very presence at the execution will anger the legion to madness and rally the slaves, perhaps to fight once more."

Vesper found herself nodding along with his words as she drew in a deep breath. When he was finished, she looked up, coming to a decision. "Well," she began, her gaze taking them all in. "It looks like we have one more battle in the arena; let's make it a good one."

"A battle?" said Jacob, frowning at them. "No, no, a distraction, followed by a quick escape amid the chaos."

Vesper opened herself to the weave, gooseflesh running over her body as torrents of Ase flowed through her, and the room was cast in a bright white light, when the concentric patterns on her arms began to glow. "No more running," she said. "My control of Ase is greater than it has ever been, and it's time we took full advantage of my growing strength."

"Daughter, that is not how it works. You cannot call bolts of lightning from the sky and belch fire without reality fighting back; those days are long past. Rome, in their conquest to control the physical world, has changed the spiritual one too. We cannot perform the miracles we once did."

"I know, Mother, but that does not mean I cannot use my power to stop Commodus and his cruelty, not when so many lives are at stake."

Lillith slid closer to her, her voice dropping to a whisper: "That is only because you have never lived through a backlash or witnessed the destruction. Why risk it all for a few slaves who would not care if you lived or died?"

"It is a risk I am willing to take, Mother," she said, her thoughts going to Linus and all the other slaves who had sought freedom, only to have it snapped away from them. "And we take the risk because I know now what it means to be a slave and to be free once more. If we succeed, more will be free, and the world will be a better place, not just for a chosen few with wealth and power, but for everyone!"

EIGHT

THE BEST-LAID PLANS

Narcissus fell back on the thick grass, his body spent, his hairy chest heaving. "You have to give me a few moments before I can do that again."

"Again! Have you lost your mind! I can't do that again," laughed Vesper, falling on the grass beside him with a beaming smile on her face, looking just as elated as he felt.

"Oh, thank the gods!" he said, wiping beads of sweat from his brow.

He closed his eyes for a moment, enjoying the sounds and smells of night, a smile creasing his face when she snuggled in close to him. They had spent the rest of the day planning their attack on the Colosseum and now had retired to Senator Sabinus's garden after a simple evening meal of olives, cheese, and bread drenched in garum. Narcissus usually found the popular fish sauce too pungent for his tastes, but the senator's cook had a more subtle version of it that was not too rough on his tongue, and he had overeaten, much to his regret, when Vesper had started kissing his neck, and then against his protests, dragged him to a secluded section of the garden where they wouldn't be heard or seen. "For a proper Ose girl, you seem to have lost all of your sense of inhibition."

"You're a bad influence," she joked, her small fist connecting with the wound on his ribs when she punched him.

"Careful" he said, his face taking on a sour look when a jolt of pain shot through his side. "The wound is still sensitive, even after your healing."

"Apologies, I wish that I could do more, but my mother could only describe how to use Ase to heal a wound."

Narcissus passed a hand over his flank where Jacob's blade had pierced him, shaking his head in amazement. "I am grateful; the wound feels as if it happened weeks ago, not today."

"For the first time I feel like my skills are strong enough that I can make a difference. To truly fulfill my destiny to be Rome's djambe."

He nodded in agreement, having watched her grow in power these past months. She was confident in her abilities now, displaying talents beyond imagining. "I agree," he began, his eyes drawn to the curtain of stars glittering above them, smiling at her before continuing. "That is the only reason I am going along with this mad plan of yours."

"It will work," she said, leaning back to look at the night sky. "I used to do this with my Aunt Magda. Every day after our evening meal, she would brush or braid my hair, and we would gaze at the stars. It was always my favorite time of the day."

"I did the same with my father... a lifetime ago."

"What was he like?" she asked.

Narcissus shrugged, squeezing shut his eyes in an attempt to remember the man. "He was hard but fair, big like me. More than that, I can't remember. I was young when the Romans took me... so young that I cannot remember his face."

"And your mother?"

"It was she who blessed me with the fiery hair... and temper," he said with a wide smile. "But no more than that."

At his side, Vesper sat up, her normally brown eyes flashing with a golden hue. Through their bond he felt the thrill he knew well, the rush of energy coursing through her as she drew on the Ase in her blood and that of the weave, filling her with potential. The power to impose her will on reality to twist it to her will and desire. "I am going to try something," she said at last. "Something I have been wondering about since we began sharing our strength." Vesper's voice fell to a whisper, and she began to sing, her words deep and somber, thrumming through the garden in low tones that made him think of lonely planes under a cold, moonless sky.

"What?"

She said nothing more, but Narcissus was suddenly cold and then hot, his heart beating faster and then slowing, a jumble of emotions rushing through his mind while she continued to sing the song under her breath. He raised a hand to stop her when, with a rush, the world around him shifted. "Do you see," she said, her voice shaking, her body beside him stiff as a board.

"What am I seeing?" he gasped, blinking in wonder when his eyes were drawn to the thin lines of emerald and gold that glowed bright against the dark of night.

"Look up," she whispered.

"By the gods," he said, his words catching in his throat. "What is it?"

Vesper's fingers locked with his, and a pulse of joy came through their bond that made him want to sing at the top of his lungs. "This is the weave," she began, "at least part of it. This is what I see when I look at the sky, how the Ose and the chosen see the world... when we choose to."

Narcissus lost track of the infinite threads of light that flowed from the garden, stretching to the night sky. In the distance there were more, more than he could ever count, flickering every shade imaginable. "It's all connected," he said in a deep rumble. "You, me, the plants, people, even people I don't know, I can see it."

"All of us," she said, nodding beside him. "This is the weave that makes up all of humanity, the tapestry of mankind. Past, present, and future. And if you follow certain threads, we can connect with those we love even if they are no longer with us."

He opened his mouth to speak but fell silent when she took his hand and guided him, following a pair of threads that flowed to a distant pair of figures on the tapestry that grew larger the longer he stared at them. "Father!" he said, drawing in a sharp breath through his teeth when he realized their images were dim compared to the others around them. "Mother!"

"Yes," she said, rubbing a soft hand up and down his arms, her eyes full of sympathy, "but there are more, many more," she said.

He could see that the threads connecting them to him were connected to others, familiar-looking men and women, many of them with the same fiery red hair, the same eyes and pale skin. "These are my kin, my clan."

"You are not alone," said Vesper in a hoarse voice as the images in the sky faded.

Narcissus tore himself away from the heavens to find that she was trembling, and her head was bowed with fatigue. "Apologies, that was more difficult than expected."

"You have given me a wondrous gift," he said, looking once more to the night sky. "I have spent all my years in Rome thinking I was alone, a clan of one, but now I have you. I know that my family lives, and that one day I may see them again."

Vesper leaned against him once more, her fingers dancing among the hairs on his chest, sending shivers of pleasure up and down his body and gooseflesh rising on his arms. "After the battle in the arena, once we find Lucilla, after we free Linus and the others, we can go to them. You can see your homeland once more."

"That's not possible... is it?"

She rolled on top of him, cupping his face in her hands. "Everything is possible when we're together," she said, her lips brushing his. "Now that we are free, nothing can stop us."

Narcissus stared deep into her eyes, doubting her words at first, thinking it impossible that after so many years he could go home. "Nothing can stop us," he said, pressing his lips to hers, their bodies moving together despite his protests of only a few minutes ago: lust, love, and hope driving them to greater heights, to greater joy.

NINE
WANDERING

Lucilla ran, shambling half-blind in the cloying gloom, seeing only when the sky was brightened by jagged flashes of cobalt lightning, offering her the occasional sight of her goal, a series of towering mountains in the distance. When she had stepped off the cobblestone path onto the bone-chilling, barren earth, she had expected the damned to be waiting for her. Instead, she found only darkness and the voices, the haunting cacophony of whispers and distant wails calling her, urging her to come to them, to find salvation in those she once loved.

The cold seeped into her bones, and after a time, she lost all sense of time or scale, only knowing that she had to run, to race forward one step at a time, or she would certainly die. She walked alone in the dark, unsure and full of doubt, the constant whispers keeping her nerves on edge, the next, when the sky was filled with brilliant flashes of lightning, leaving her feeling small, alone, and insignificant, twisting her hands in terror.

The ground shook with a boom of thunder when the hairs on the back of her neck stood on end, a chill running up and down her spine when a familiar voice touched her ear. "My love, come to me."

"Lucius," she whispered, her spine stiffening while her stomach clenched in knots. Lucius, her first husband, had died on the way back to Rome, food poisoning she was told by a Praetorian guardsmen, who had escorted the body back to Rome for funeral rights. When they had shown her his emaciated body, black and shrunken, her sanity had cracked. Lucilla had spent months on end, lost in the house of Bacchus, drowning in wine and pleasures of the flesh, dreaming of a final touch with him. Now, in this barren place, she once again heard the deep timber of his voice, the kindness, and she yearned for his hands on her, his lips on hers. "Is it really you?"

"Of course, my love," said the voice she knew so well, from off to the side now. "I have waited for so long, to hold you in my arms once again."

Lucilla spun in a circle, ears straining as the voices grew in number, all of them echoing words of love and yearning, calling to her. Narrowing her eyes, she gripped her temples, desperate to see beyond the cloying gloom. "Stop! Please, stop," she shouted in a shaking voice, wishing for a weapon of some kind. "Lucius, if it's you, please, my love, show yourself."

A distant flash lit up the sky, and she clutched her chest in panic when she caught a glimpse of a throng of blank faces surrounding her, a horde of the dead beyond counting, shuffled closer with each breath. "No!" she shouted when a pale hand, the color of ash, reached out from the gloom, fingers hungry for her throat. "Get back!" At its touch, a brilliant flash blinded her, and a piercing scream erupted from her throat. Panic took hold, and Lucilla ran, her mind a jumble of screams and flashing light, while numbing cold threatened to shatter her bones each time a shade tore at her, their haunting wails growing louder as she pressed through. Lucilla did not know how she survived, but after an eternity of running, she somehow staggered free, finding herself in a circle of cold light near the edge of a slope that was covered in jagged rocks.

In the distance, Lucilla could still hear the shades calling to her, Lucius louder than the rest, but the light was brighter here, the cool glow of the mountains somehow holding the shades back. Shuddering in relief, she climbed a little higher, clawing and scraping with bloodied fingers while her breath rasped in her ears, not stopping until she reached a tiny perch of flat rock. Here, she could still hear the voices, but they were distant, easier to push from her mind.

Scurrying away from the edge of her tiny plateau, she pressed her back against the rock wall, for the first time since she stepped off the cobblestone path, letting her guard down, her shoulders falling in relief. She stayed like that for a time, in a state of panic, taking in gulps of stale air to calm her racing heart, flinching each time thunder boomed in the distance, or lightning flashed across the sky, until she at last fell into a fitful slumber, her sleep disturbed by dreams of Mother Ayaba arguing with Magnus, their words full of spite, with Magnus finally storming off, vanishing down the cobblestone path, to where, she could not say.

She came awake with a start, the faint glow surrounding her still present, sure that a warm breeze just had caressed her pale skin. Rubbing sleep from her eyes, she dragged herself over to the edge of her tiny refuge, taking advantage of the flashes of lightning to survey her surroundings. Lucilla bit her lip when she saw that the damned were still present, huddled in numbers beyond counting at the base of the jagged mountains. Narrowing her eyes, she searched the horizon for the cobblestone path, hoping beyond hope that she could somehow make her way back, cursing herself when she saw nothing but barren, lifeless soil. "If the damned don't get me, thirst and hunger surely will," she said, gasping as she rolled on her back, realizing that the pale glow came from the shallow cuts Magnus had carved along her arms and chest during his failed ritual.

"What in the name of the gods is this?" she muttered, removing her filth-streaked stola, her curiosity greater than her need for modesty. She had watched Mother Ayaba perform the same ritual repeatedly, carving the same symbols on the arms of every senator she had introduced the old woman to, and each time the Sandawei matron had finished, by plunging a bone-handled dagger in the men's hearts. Now those symbols decorated her own flesh, yet somehow the ritual was incomplete, and the symbols were casting a pale light.

Lucilla was about to inspect them further when a peal of thunder sounded directly overhead, forcing her to throw her hands over her head as a shower of tiny stone shards rained down on her, one of them cutting her just below her right eye, leaving a tear-shaped droplet on her pale cheek. Cursing her luck, she picked up her grime-covered stola, ripping away the hem of the garment and using it to staunch the bleeding. The sky was bright once more, and Lucilla caught sight of herself and began to laugh. It was a small giggle at first, then a deep-throated laugh, and after a few moments, her whole body was shaking with laughter until her belly hurt from the effort of it, her heart full of joy. Today she had made one of the few decisions that she had ever made and had ended up naked, crying blood on the side of a mountain while being watched by the damned: for some reason it made her laugh.

Wiping the remaining blood off her face, she dressed, intending to climb as high as she could. She had only managed a short distance when a whisper reached her, making the fine hair on her arms stand on end. "Do not go up there, my love," said a shade, its voice taking on hints of the husband she once knew. "Only death awaits."

Lucilla stopped climbing, almost falling when her grip faltered. "Then I shall die," she said to herself, or to the shade, she couldn't be sure. Despite her defiance, the whispers continued, growing fainter the higher she climbed, pushing her to climb faster to escape them. Lucilla pushed herself beyond her limits, ignoring her shaking arms and legs, enduring the pain and the blood flowing freely from the cuts on her hands and knees, defying her every instinct that told her to go back, to return to the gilded cages that had been her life. She began to climb faster when she saw another plateau not far above, to her right, adrenaline giving her a strength beyond what she thought possible.

Scaling along the near flat face of the slope, she shifted ever so slowly to her goal, shuffling along higher and higher while she pressed her body flat against the jagged stone, her skin bruising with each step. She was almost at her goal and reached out, nearly falling when she realized the hand hold was just out of reach. Catching her balance, Lucilla changed tactics, leaning forward as far as she could while reaching once more, only to curse when she slipped, her breath catching in her throat when she fell a few inches, the luck of the gods saving her when she found another hand hold, just below her. Clutching at the rock wall in desperation, she shook with wide-eyed terror. Looking over the cliff face, she hunted for another way, any way to reach her goal, but the longer she looked, the more despair set in, and she knew there was only one way up. "I have to jump," she croaked, wanting to let go, but she didn't dare, not after coming so far. Reaching down deep, delving deep to memories full of hurt and anger, screaming them loud like a battle cry: "I curse you all. I curse you, Brother, for your arrogance. I curse you, Father, for leaving the empire to your weakest child, and I curse you, Lucius, for leaving me alone in this world!"

With everything she had left, she leapt, screeching like an eagle as she flew, a shout of victory escaping her lips when she caught the rock hold and swung herself onto the plateau, laughing and crying from the sheer joy of being alive when she fell on her hands and knees, not caring for the pain, only grateful to be alive. Rolling onto her back, she wanted nothing more than a moment to catch her breath, only to fall silent when a slow rhythmic beating combined with a hypnotic twang reached her ear. Thinking quickly, she flipped onto her belly and was greeted with the sight of a large cave mouth, and from it, a warm, flickering glow called to her. She was not alone.

TEN
VULGAR DISPLAYS

Vesper crossed an invisible line, and the taint was there once more, her belly churning with waves of nausea the moment they passed Trajan's market at the edge of the inner city. The massive brick shopping arcade where almost any good or service could be purchased, no matter how rare or exotic. When she had lived at the ludus, she had grown accustomed to the filth that permeated the weave, the corruption, but they had been away long enough that she had almost forgotten it. Now she reeled against the oily feel on her skin and the rancid taste in the back of her throat. "I had forgotten the smell of this place," she said to Jacob, shuddering from the cold rain whipping past her, the woolen palla she had thrown over her shoulders, doing little to keep the deluge from soaking her to the skin. "And I doubt I will ever get used to the cold."

The former medicus glanced up at the iron-gray sky, pulling tight the oversized cloak he wore to hide the scarred leather armor he wore underneath. "It has always been a foul place," he said, his lips turning down into a harsh frown. "As to the weather, this is nothing. You should see Britannia. It rains like this at the height of summer and doesn't get much warmer."

Vesper frowned at him, her brows coming together. "And people live there? Willingly?"

Jacob laughed, and for an instant, she caught a glimpse of the pleasant man she remembered. The former medicus had saved her life, tended to grievous wounds, and she was having a hard seeing his as an assassin, "I suppose they do," he said with a shrug. "I have spent more time in the northern reaches of the empire than I ever wanted to, and almost none in the African provinces from where you hail. Don't you have a winter season?"

"Not like this," she shouted, dodging past a wagon loaded with jugs of oil, its heavy wooden wheels making a terrible racket on the cobblestone road. "It's warm, like the rest of the year, just wet."

"Careful, there is a patrol up ahead," he snapped, picking up his pace so he passed the legionnaires on the other side of a loaded wagon, concealing him from their sight.

"You're good at this," she said, following his lead, step for step.

"This mad endeavor will be for nothing if they spot us, worse still if you get caught."

Vesper nodded in agreement. It was one of the reasons she traveled with Jacob, while Narcissus entered the city after them with Lillith, much to the big man's annoyance. Commodus had proclaimed them to be leaders of the slave revolt, and as such, their descriptions were known to every legionnaire in the city and beyond, so it was safer to travel apart. "I doubt anyone will notice us in this crowd, certainly not with this rain."

"Just keep your head down," said Jacob, threading his way through the crowded street. Vesper followed his instructions, bowing her head against the elements while trying to blend in as they passed through the Forum Romanum, a large rectangular plaza that was once the heart of Roman public life. At the height of the republic, the grand square was used for public discussions, criminal trials, and elections, but with the advent of the imperial age, the open square was surrounded by important government buildings of all kinds. Vesper caught herself gawking at the towering pillars that were evenly spaced, each of them made of fine marble and topped with golden statues of Rome's praetors and generals, men who achieved enough glory for the empire to be deified or honored here. A shudder of fear ran through her when they passed the Curia Julia, the seat of the Roman Senate, where Commodus, in his madness, had sentenced her and Narcissus to fight to the death, and she was grateful when they passed through the victory arch of the great Caesar Augustus, leaving the square and the memory behind.

When she caught sight of the Colosseum in the distance, her shoulders hunched up, and the tension returned just as quickly as it had passed. "I don't know if I can do this," she muttered to Jacob, walking close enough to him so that only he could hear her words. "I've never tried drawing on so much Ase on a grand scale, especially when mired in the filth of the city's taint."

"I don't understand your witchcraft, but it's too late. Our plans hinge on your skills," he said with a smirk, his focus on their destination never wavering. "Besides, having doubts is good. Only fools walk into a lion's den without fearing the lion."

"Gratitude," said Vesper, the tension easing in her shoulders the more he spoke.

"Don't thank me; we've done nothing yet. Focus on the mission; prepare yourself, and follow my lead, no matter how bizarre."

"Of course," said Vesper, craning her neck to marvel at the size of the great Colosseum as they drew closer. Even after having battled on its sands, knowing what kinds of horrors were done within its walls, she was still in awe of its majesty, its craftsmanship. Pushing away her doubt as they approached one of the many entrances, she did as she was told. Drawing on the innate Ase coursing through her, Vesper formed a razor-sharp gladius and leather scabbard on her hip, concealing the conjured weapon under her cloak.

At the empty gate, Vesper counted four men, rough-looking legionnaires that looked to be of low rank, the type of men who were more for show than anything, their presence meant to keep the rowdier citizens and slaves in line during events, such as today's executions.

"You're too early," said a short legionnaire to Jacob, rubbing the bridge of a nose that looked like it had been broken more than once. "The magistrate has ordered that the gates open midmorning, no earlier."

Vesper blinked in surprise when Jacob was suddenly hunched over, his voice cracking and tired. "I beg of you; have pity on an old man," he said, coughing into his hand. "I am not well, and my sight fails me. I fear the gods will summon me to the afterlife soon. I only wish for a place near the front, or I won't see a thing."

"My dominus just wishes to enjoy the games, one last time," said Vesper, bowing her head, instinctively playing along.

The legionnaire frowned at them, taking a step back. "Go die somewhere else, old man; we don't have time for your foolishness."

"I have denarii," said Jacob in a desperate tone, jangling a small pouch in front of the shorter man. "Maybe even a little extra for your kindness?" Another legionnaire behind the first licked his lips, pulling his cohort back to whisper in his ear.

"And what about her?" he said at last, dry-washing his hands.

Jacob coughed again, hacking and choking until finally clutching his chest, gasping for breath. "Just a slave girl who sees to an old man's comfort. There is more than enough coin to cover both of us."

The legionnaire covered his mouth with his cloak, the red garment stained brown and tattered along the edges. "Fine, fine!" he said, bouncing the pouch in his hand, "Just get out of my sight, and don't make any trouble, or you will see the afterlife sooner than you think. Now move along, before our patience wears thin."

The assassin knuckled his forehead, and they moved past the guardsmen, his shuffling gait returning to its long stride once they were deeper in the darkness and out of sight. "Roman scum," he spat, glaring over his shoulder with a frown on his narrow face. "They would sell their own mothers for enough denarii."

"They're not all like that," said Vesper. "Lucilla and her husband—"

"She sat idly by in the emperor's box for years as slaves were murdered before her eyes," he said. "She did nothing while her husband and father burned nations to the ground and then crucified soldiers for trying to protect their homes, enslaving women and children all for the glory of the empire."

"I'm sorry," said Vesper in a small voice.

"Sorry for what?" he asked, taking them down a side corridor that led down a sloping ramp.

"For your hate and pain," she said. "For what the empire has done to you."

Jacob stopped in his tracks, and Vesper gripped tight to her gladius, fearing he was about to attack when he spun on his heel to face her. "Don't talk about things you know nothing about. I have no pain in my heart. I don't deserve or want your pity. I only desire to punish those so richly deserving of death. Do you understand?"

They stood in silence, their eyes locked together. Vesper could see nothing in his eyes, no hint of anger or hatred, just steady calm, and that frightened her the most. "Of course, my apologies for thinking otherwise. I am not here to judge you."

"Good, good," said Jacob, cocking his head as if he had expected a different answer. "Now come along, before those legionnaires realize we are not searching for seats. Jacob turned on his heel and resumed their descent down the curving tunnel.

Despite the cool temperatures above, beneath the Colosseum, it was a furnace, and by the time her ear caught the occasional grunt, scream, or snap of the whip, she was ready to throw off her leather vest, tunic, and cloak as the heat became unbearable. They came to a large opening dominated by cages, and she gagged on the odor of unwashed bodies, her eyes going wide when a sea of humanity stretched out before her. Vesper cursed under her breath, having lost count of how many men were huddling like animals in the filthy space, heavy iron chains connecting them by their wrists and ankles.

"By Olodumare, how are we going to find Lucilla in all this mess, much less free any of these people."

"I think we'll find out sooner rather than later," said Jacob, pointing with his chin at a tired-looking legionnaire with a heavily lined face and deep circles under his eyes. Even in the dark, Vesper could see that his leather armor was worn and cracked along its edges, while his cloak looked like it hadn't been washed in months.

"No killing," she whispered to Jacob, seeing how the assassin shifted his stance. "You promised."

"We'll see," he whispered out of the side of his mouth, his hands invisible under his cloak.

"You're not supposed to be down here," said the legionnaire, without a hint of emotion on his face, resting a hand on the hilt of his gladius. "Return to your seats, or I'll see to it that you're executed along with the prisoners later today.

"Apologies," said Vesper, stepping forward. "We are—"

"The hypogeum is closed to the public," he growled, unsheathing a portion of his gladius to show the naked steel. "No one is supposed to be down here, leave!"

"Apologies" said Jacob, spinning in place.

Vesper blinked, and in a blur of motion almost too quick to see, Jacob was suddenly at the legionary's side, holding up him up. "Help me, quickly, before any of the other guards notice." She dashed forward to help, catching the falling man on his other side, staring in wonder at the ugly red welt growing on the side of the man's temple.

"What did you do? Is he dead?" she asked, helping Jacob pull the man back up the ramp and out of sight.

The assassin lowered him down, propping the limp body against the rough stone wall so it looked like he was sleeping. "Not dead," he said, showing her an arm's-length leather strap that bulged on one end. "But he will wish he was. He'll wake in a few hours with a splitting headache, not remembering much; even his own name might be a blur. You'll find that a good solid knock on the head can do wonders in making people forget they ever saw you."

"So, what now?" she said, casting a worried glance at the leather weapon. "How do we find Lucilla or Linus in this mess?"

"We find the woman first," said Jacob. "There are fewer and would be kept apart. The last thing Commodus would want would be slaves enjoying the pleasures of the flesh, not when they have vexed him so."

"Agreed," she said, knowing how petty the emperor was, having lived through enough of his antics. They returned to the foul-smelling underbelly of the Colosseum, snaking their way through the shackled masses, ignoring the reaching hands and pleading voices. Vesper's heart broke when she saw the battered bruising on their faces, the welts on their backs, and she was grateful that the dark hid her shame for not being able to free them right away.

"Keep your emotions under control," said Jacob in a harsh whisper. "It will do us nor them any good if they run for the exits now. The legion will only cut them down, causing more senseless deaths."

Vesper sucked in a shuddering breath, gritting her teeth to harden her heart. "I know, I know, but patience has never been my strength."

They made their way to the opposite side of the underground complex, squeezing around wooden platforms attached to winch and pulley systems that could lift them to the main level of the Colosseum to replace parts of the grounds with different scenery, elevate exotic animals in cages, or even provide battlefield fortifications to reenact many of Rome's ancient wars. "Here," said Jacob, cocking his head in an attempt to get a better view around the heavy cloth curtain that vanished into the darkness above their heads.

Vesper pushed past him, entering a better lit area that had an odd mix of cages filled with female slaves, along with big cats of all kinds. Scanning for Lucilla, she noticed predators familiar and foreign. Male lions with their shaggy golden manes were caged beside black-spotted cheetahs, while bizarre animals that she was unfamiliar with stalked back and forth in cages, casting hungry looks at them. "Lucilla," she shouted suddenly, racing toward a cage holding a tallish woman with long, brown hair, whose stola, despite being covered in grime, was trimmed purple and gold.

"Please take me home, Domina. I-I can't take anymore," stammered the woman, shaking in terror when Vesper kneeled beside her. "I will be good. Never will I touch your things again. I swear by the gods." Staring at her vacant eyes and hollow cheeks, it was clear that she had no clue who Vesper was. The woman was some unlucky slave, and not her friend.

"She's not an escaped slave," said Vesper, taking the woman's soft hands in hers. "She's never done a moment of labor in her life."

Above her Jacob looked down his nose at them, clenching and unclenching his fist. "I'm sure many a Roman has taken this opportunity to purge unwanted slaves from their service."

Vesper stood, wiping away dirt and grit from her knees. "Surely she has value. Why not just sell her? Why cast her away like this?"

"Some don't care for the coin," said Jacob with a shrug. "But from the looks of her, she was some patrician woman's handmaid for a time. She must have done something to upset her domina, and this is her punishment."

Vesper's blood boiled, and she ground her teeth in a flash of anger. "Let's find Linus and Lucilla... before I do something I will regret."

Jacob's thin shoulders shook with silent laughter as he showed her the whites of his teeth in a feral smile. "And there it is," he said.

"What? What's so funny?"

"You feel such anger for one cast-out slave," he began, his smile fading. "Imagine the weight of an entire people cast out. Thousands of mothers, fathers, and children, torn from their homes, their only crime... being born a Jew."

"And you've let it consume you," she said, drawing in a deep breath, then letting the anger out in a slow exhale through her mouth. The lines of Jacob's thin face, the haunted look in his eyes painted the picture of a man consumed by a lifetime of anger, of hate. "Let hate ruin you until there is nothing left but the hunger for revenge."

"It will be you one day," he snapped, turning away from her to keep searching. "When the pain of this life has burned the hope from you."

"Let's just find those we are here for," she said, praying to Olodu-mare that he was wrong. Vesper lost track of time while they waded through the sad sea of humanity, searching for their friends while avoiding the few legionaries in the area, a sense of impending doom and panic playing havoc with her nerves the longer they searched. Throwing up her arms in frustration, she fought the urge to scream out their names, knowing that calling attention to herself would only cause more trouble than it was worth.

The faint rattle of chains followed by deep-throated, commanding shouts cut short their search, and Vesper cursed under her breath. "We're out of time," she said, stopping beside him.

"Then we go with our contingency," he said, his face like stone. "Are Narcissus and Lillith close?"

Vesper closed her eyes for a moment, feeling her way past the rotted pattern that permeated the city, a smile growing on her face when she felt the familiar warmth that flowed through their bond, that Narcissus was close. "He's here, above us near the entrance."

"Good," said the assassin, standing on his toes and craning his neck to catch a glimpse at what was happening near the exit to the hypogeum. "We will blend in with the slaves when they are taken onto the sands. Hopefully we will have a better chance to see Linus and Lucilla in the light of day."

She could only nod as the darkness was banished by a group of cohorts carrying lanterns, dragging the captives to their feet, while a dark-skinned legionnaire, with a square jaw and a massive beak of a nose, put a barbed whip to work, driving those in chains to move. Vesper bowed her head, following the long line of captives as they were brought up through the sloped passage that led to the sands of the Colosseum, her teeth chattering as beads of cold rain rolled down her temples. Despite the weather, the massive amphitheater was full of cheering citizens and slaves, all hungry for a spectacle of blood.

Ignoring the cheering masses, Vesper felt her way through the bond she shared with Narcissus, a smile creeping onto her face when she caught a glimpse of his massive frame that dwarfed all those sitting beside him, including Lillith, whose beautiful face was turned up in disgust as she cast hateful glances at the lowborn of Rome surrounding her.

"I see Linus," said Jacob in a hurried tone, a tiny crack of joy appearing on his face.

Vesper tore her eyes away from Narcissus to look past the hundreds of slaves crowding the sands to find the old gladiator at the head of a column of chained men, apart from the others, standing tall and strong, close to the emperor's box. "He looks well despite it all," she said, looking him up and down, surprised to see that his sun-kissed skin had faded to a reddish pink. He appeared fit, his sinewy body looking lean and strong. "All of the men with him, do."

"My brother was never one to give in, or give up," said Jacob, his voice full of pride. "It looks like he's organized resistance, even bound in chains."

Vesper opened her mouth to speak when a horn sounded, a single peal, loud and clear, that pierced the din of the murmuring crowds. All eyes turned to the emperor's box as the note faded, waiting for the auditor to announce the start of the executions. Instead, Commodus himself stood at the forefront of the marble podium, the assembled Romans, gasping in awe when they saw that he wore nothing but a loincloth to cover his athletic frame, while his familiar lion's mane adorned his shoulders. "By Olodumare," she gasped, shaking her head.

"Citizens of Rome," he boomed, raising his arms in a V, his chiseled body like that of an Olympian, glistening in the rain. "I, Caesar Augustus Lucius Aelius Aurelius Commodus, offer today's games in honor of our communal sacrifice. We Romans, in our kindness, opened our homes and hearts to these traitors assembled on the sands before you, but they chose to spurn our generosity, our kindness!"

"Kindness," muttered Vesper under her breath, bowing her head and shifting her vision to the world beyond, recoiling in disgust by the tattered weave that bent and twisted before her eyes.

Jacob leaned in close to whisper in her ear, weaving his hands in front of him. "Now would be a good time to perform whatever trickery you plan to do."

"It's coming," she said, sucking in a deep breath while she drew on the Ase in her blood, spreading her fingers wide and then linking them together. "I've only drawn on this type of Ase twice before, and it was always during life-or-death moments. Jacob continued to press her, but she ignored his frantic voice, the driving rain, even Commodus droning on about the glories of Rome. She had done this on the night her Aunt Magda had died, and then once more on the day she almost died battling the pair of gold-painted dwarves. Vesper fumbled as she reached out, feeling as though she were trying to hold running water with open fingers, the power slipping through her hands in torrents. Then, with a gasp, there was a sudden rush of life, an intoxicating joy that made her want to weep as she pulled the very essence of life from those all around her. It was a trickle at first, and she fought the urge to take it all, instead, expanding her reach, until she drew on the life force of all the men and women crowding her on the sands.

"Vesper! We are out of time!" said Jacob, falling against her as the crowd surged, screams reaching her ears, even deep in focus.

A calloused hand grabbed her roughly by the upper arms, and a stranger's deep voice reached her ear. "Up to the front with you."

Ignoring the voice, Vesper drew on a deep well of memory of her people, the Ose. Knowledge of Ase that had grown since her gift from Eshu, the primordial loa she had met months ago. With a shout of triumph, she raised a clawed hand to the heavens, releasing a portion of the Ase she was holding, with a shudder of exhilaration. She opened her eyes to meet those of the legionnaire holding her arm, and he shrank away, covering his head in panic as a peal of thunder shook the great Colosseum. "No," she said, his eyes shooting open wide when crooked fingers of lightning flashed across the sky. "Never again! Your time is at an end." The concentric patterns covering her body glowed bright against her dark skin as Vesper focused the remainder of the Ase coursing through her. She pushed forward her will, intent on shattering the chains binding the slaves when a force stopped her, her breath blasting from her lungs as if she had slammed into an invisible wall, holding back her Ase.

From the emperor's box, a wild laugh pierced the boom and crash of thunder as Commodus appeared, bearing a massive club over his shoulder. All around him the shadows deepened, and Vesper understood that it was him who was channeling some unseen force, that his will was opposing her own. "Come, then, Ose witch," he shouted, his face aglow with a maniacal smile. "Let us finish this once and for all: come and die at my hand so that I never have to deal with you again."

Vesper answered his challenge with a smile, drawing on more Ase from the thousands of souls filling the Colosseum, pressing her will against his. "Once and for all," she answered, her shouts loud enough to shatter stone. "To the afterlife with you!"

ELEVEN
TEMPEST

Narcissus rose to his feet, flinching along with the rest of the Colosseum when peals of thunder echoed across the sky while fat drops of rain fell in a blinding torrent. At his side Lillith did the same, staring dumbfounded at Vesper and Commodus as they faced off against one another. "Let's finish this," he said, balling his fists.

"Agreed," said Lillith, a feral grin crossing her beautiful features as she drew an ornate gladius from her hip, hefting a shield taken off her back adorned with the same concentric patterns that Vesper had on her arms.

"Don't stop, crush everyone in your path," he grunted, his eyes never leaving Vesper, who stood stock still in the middle of the Colosseum. "Get Linus out with as many others as you can. Leave the rest to Vesper and I."

Lillith nodded to him, hefting her shield. "Go!"

Narcissus bellowed an ear-piercing battle cry, vaulting down the sloped steps in twos and threes like a madman, until finally leaping from the seating onto the sands, with a grunt. He took his first legionnaires from behind, crashing into their phalanx and throwing it into chaos while the men scattered in all directions. Before they could recover, the giant Celt grabbed the man closest to him, crushing the hapless legionnaire's windpipe with a meaty hand. In the next breath, he tore the shield away from another man just getting to his feet, kicking out his legs from under him and then using the edge of it to pierce his breastbone, spilling bright red blood onto the sands.

"Javelins, from the left," shouted Lillith, appearing at his side, burying her gladius in the shoulder of a legionnaire still on his knees.

Spinning on his heel, Narcissus ducked under the bloodied shield just as a volley of the steel-tipped javelins clattered off its wooden surface. "Cowards," he seethed, his blood boiling with rage as a surge of adrenaline coursed through his veins.

Despite the chaos around them, Lillith smiled with glee as jagged arcs of lightning flashed across the sky. "If you saw your face, you would be afraid too," she laughed, blocking a clumsy strike from a legionnaire whose leather armor bulged around his thick middle, her quick parry neatly slicing his throat open.

"They should be afraid," he growled, losing himself in the violence, animal instinct taking over. Like a beast, he plowed into those who opposed him, deflecting thrusting swords with the fine steel bracers on his forearms while shattering faces with his fists, breaking bones with his elbows and knees, striking fear into the men facing him. Around them, the darkness deepened as the storm grew, and in the distance, he caught sight of Vesper standing in an empty circle, her face locked in concentration, not having moved since the start of the storm, those around her battling as if she didn't exist.

"They battle with their very wills, with Ase," shouted Lillith, pointing to Commodus, who did the same, his face a mask of stone while he focused all his attention on Vesper.

Narcissus bent his knees, springing toward a single legionnaire who charged at him, the impact of shields dwarfing the thunder as they slammed into one another. The other man was thrown back like a rag doll from the blow, landing on his back with a deep groan, his eyes rolling back in his head. "Can we help her?" he said, catching another legionnaire's spear between his arm and body while slamming his head into the bridge of his nose, flattening it to a pulp.

Lillith shook her head, her dark eyes wide with worry as lightning began to strike among shackled slaves and soldiers alike, killing indiscriminately. "No, but I fear what will happen. I've never felt this much Ase being channeled in one place."

"I thought your abilities were gone," he said, slamming his shield into another man and sending him reeling.

"They are," she said, ducking past a thrown javelin, "but can't you feel it? The hum in the air, like the world is about to fly apart."

He stopped for a heartbeat, his massive chest heaving as he opened himself to the connection between himself and Vesper, gasping in shock when he sensed what was coursing through her. At most times he felt her emotion, joy and sadness, hate and love. If he focused hard enough, he could feel what she felt, the heat of the sun on her skin, the taste of wine on her tongue, but now, it was beyond his understanding. She vibrated like a cord drawn taut as if she were about to shatter into a thousand pieces of glass. Most of all he felt fear and a desperate sense that she was trying to hold on to something, what, he couldn't say. "She's terrified, losing control."

"Then we have to stop this, before it's too late, not just for her but for all of us," said Lillith, dancing forward to catch a killing blow meant for Narcissus, with her shield, her gladius spitting out like a viper's tongue, taking the legionnaire's eye and sending him falling back.

Narcissus looked around, his jaw falling open when he saw that many of the slaves were throwing themselves against the legionnaires, fighting with chains and shackles. "I will end this," he said, finding what he was searching for among the fallen, a still intact javelin. Leaning back on one leg, he drew back his arm, taking aim as he sprung forward, hurling the javelin with all his might. Narcissus held his breath as the razor-sharp weapon flew straight toward its target, Commodus himself. A smile came to his face when his throw landed true, striking the emperor's chest, sending him falling from sight.

The sky brightened for a heartbeat, the rain slacking. "Did you get him. Is he dead?" asked Lillith, a smile creeping onto her face as the arena fell silent. Ignoring her, he took a step toward Vesper, only for his breath to catch in his throat as Commodus reappeared on the podium holding a bloodied javelin, his taut stomach glistening red from a deep gash along his side.

"No," said Narcissus, swallowing hard as Commodus hurled the javelin, blinking in confusion when a web of pain spread from his belly and out his back as he fell to his knees, warm blood spilling onto his hands as he clutched at the weapon in his gut. Kneeling in front of him, Lillith appeared, words spilling from her mouth but not reaching his ears, her face twisted by worry. He tried waving her away, muttering that he was fine, that he just needed a moment to catch his breath, but only a groan escaped his lips as he fell to his side. Narcissus wanted to close his eyes, to rest, but she kept shaking him. With his last ounce of strength, he pushed her away, his sight fading as a peaceful silence descended on him, his last thoughts being of Vesper and her smile, and then... nothing.

TWELVE
DESTINY

Vesper threw her arms up in victory, shouting in triumph when the javelin slammed into Commodus, and the barrier holding back her will vanishing with him as he fell from sight. The bottled torrents of Ase coursing through her body exploded suddenly in a fountain of power. A shockwave of Ase exploded from her, hurling bodies back while shattering the iron shackles of every slave in the arena, grinding the metal to dust. The smile on her face lasted for only a moment, replaced by a look of wide-eyed shock when Commodus reappeared with only a faint line of crimson on his flank, his arm cocked to hurl the javelin that had driven him back. Vesper clenched when he threw, expecting to be impaled. Instead, she spun on her heel when the lethal weapon hissed over her shoulder, gasping, despite being untouched, jagged arcs of pain radiated outward from her belly, and she found herself clutching a wound that was not there. "Narcissus," she shouted, taking a single step toward him, only to be frozen in place, her breath catching in her throat when an invisible force slammed into her. She turned to find Commodus's dark gaze focused on her, a torrential gale pummeling against her, forcing Vesper to use every ounce of Ase she could draw upon just to stay on her feet.

The towering emperor hefted his club on his shoulder before leaping from the podium to the sands, his very presence driving slaves and soldiers to flee like gazelles, scattering to avoid a hungry lion. "You have defied us for the last time," he shouted, his deep voice somehow reaching her ear despite the howling wind and chaos all around them.

"Us?" asked Vesper, fighting the panic taking hold of her as she felt Narcissus's lifeblood spilling onto the sand.

The emperor's chiseled features broke into a smile as he spread his arms wide, flexing his rippling muscles while he turned. "Of course," he said, as a blast of hot air pushed against her and the rain no longer touched them. "We are the now fully who we were meant to be, Hercules, the son of Jupiter, a god! Bound to the flesh of the perfect man."

Vesper shifted her vision from the natural world to the world beyond, a chill running over her when she saw the tattered weave flowing all around him, while jet-black filaments writhed all around him, stretching to some void beyond her sight and understanding, making Commodus appear to be a puppet on a string, controlled by an unseen hand. "Things are not what they seem," said Vesper, raising a shaking hand to him. "You are being used, controlled."

Commodus threw his head back, a mad cackle escaping his lips. "No, little Ose. I am what I am meant to be, I have never been more alive."

He stopped an arm's length from her, and she managed a step back, stealing a glance at Narcissus, the pain in her belly giving her a faint hope that he still lived, that she could still save him. "I can help you," she said, returning her attention to the emperor, instinctively widening the circle of Ase she was drawing on from the fleeing crowds. "Together, we can cast out whatever loa is controlling you."

The stench of rot became unbearable as Commodus towered over her, and Vesper tasted bile in the back of her throat when the odor of his breath touched her nostrils. "This is why your people fell, why we

Romans rule the world, because even facing your death, you would offer to help your greatest enemy, even when none is needed."

Vesper raised her chin, casting a defiant look at him. "The loa controlling you, it will bring only death and destruction. Protecting the world is more important than our petty squabbles and foolish egos."

The towering emperor hefted his club, looking down on her. "Nothing controls me. There is nothing to save," he said, raising the club over his head. "And our petty squabbles are at an end... along with your wasted life."

"When you lie dying," said Vesper, her body vibrating with potential as Ase raced through her blood, "Remember that I gave you a chance."

Vesper didn't flinch when Commodus brought down the club, the heavy weapon whistling as it cut through the air, aiming for her skull, smiling at him when she released the Ase boiling in her blood. A blast of lightning flashed between them, the club burning to dust as Commodus staggered back, his eyes going wide when he realized he held nothing more than a blackened stump of wood. "Whore!" he shouted, throwing the now useless weapon while raising a hand to strike her.

"I warned you," said Vesper, drawing deeper from the thinning crowd, many of them staggering as she pulled on more of their life than she had intended. A shudder of pleasure pulsing through her the more she took. "You. Are. Done!" she rasped, spreading her arms wide as she released the Ase into the storm. The Colosseum shook as the world around them exploded in chaos as bolt after bolt struck from the clouds, with Commodus screaming and writhing as jagged strokes of cobalt blue pierced his heart and head, lifting the Caesar of Rome high into the air before blasting him a dozen feet away to land in a smoking heap.

Vesper gasped, her limbs trembling with exhaustion as she took a step toward Narcissus, only to halt, her instincts drawing to the fallen emperor. Staggering over to Commodus, she covered her nose with the end of her tunic to block the stench of burnt flesh as she stood over him, marveling at how the lightning had blackened and blistered his bronzed flesh. "I warned you," she said, shaking her head. Planting a foot on his chest, Vesper shoved with all her might, jumping back when a groan escaped his lips.

"Thank Olodumare I have some sense," she muttered under her breath. With the Ase in her blood singing with power, she chanted in a low voice. In the time it took to release a slow breath, creeping vines, green with the color of new life erupted from the sand beneath the fallen emperor, snaking around his prone form many times over, binding him in place.

Satisfied, Vesper pushed thoughts of Commodus from her mind, her breathing coming in anxious gulps as she raced to Narcissus's side. Kneeling at his side, she pressed her lips together in worry when warm blood washed over her hands as she gingerly probed at the wound in his belly. "Please be with me still," she said, pressing her face to his, ignoring the itch of his beard against her skin. A whisper of a breath warmed her cheek, while through their connection she sensed the faintest beating of his heart. Licking her lips, Vesper fought to remain calm while she inspected the razor-sharp javelin protruding from Narcissus's stomach, desperately searching her mind for a way to save him, to fix him. During their months in hiding, with what little instruction her mother could give her, she had learned to channel Ase to heal minor cuts and scrapes. It was easy when the wound was on the surface, when she could see the entire wound and work out how to stitch the flesh together. This was different, the weapon was deep in his gut, the tip of it protruding from his back, and she was sure that he was injured inside, with damage well beyond what she could repair.

She leaned back on her haunches, raising her face to the sky, grateful for the rain hiding the tears rolling down her face. "I will do what I must," she muttered, glancing around the near empty Colosseum, knowing that what little additional strength she could draw upon to add to her own was fleeing out the doors along with the freed

slaves, and that she would have to call on a power far more dangerous. Sucking in a deep breath, Vesper touched the series of stars
tattooed across her throat, and they began to glow when she channeled the stores of Ase in her blood through them, the stars casting an
eerie glow all around her. Throwing a clawed hand to the heavens,
she focused on an image in her mind's eye, that of a handsome man
with a knowing, twisted grin and a compact build. Raising her chin,
she called to him, shouting at the top of her lungs, "Eshu, son of
Olodumare, master trickster. I call on you to fulfill your promise.
Give me your power so that I may save this man. I offer my service,
my blood, and my life!"

Vesper waited, not daring to breathe as thunder and lightning
raged above her, the wind and rain howling through the now empty
Colosseum. When nothing happened, she cursed under her breath,
sucking in a deep breath to try once more: "Eshu, I call upon you,"
she began, pounding her fist into the sand in frustration when her
voice cracked and faltered as she began to cough. "Eshu! You
promised!"

A chill ran down her spine when the falling rain suddenly slowed
to a snail's pace, and the world around her fell silent, reality bending,
twisting, and stretching in a way that made her stomach lurch. Vesper
gasped when she touched a floating raindrop with the tip of her
finger, cocking her head in a mix of wonder and fear when the
droplet broke into smaller spheres of water, floating away ever so
slowly.

A shadow fell over her, and Vesper flinched when a hand
brushed against her shoulder. "Your wicked loa is not coming," said a
deep voice that was at once foreign and oddly familiar.

Vesper's attention snapped to a compact man glaring down at
her. He had angular, almost square features and dark skin, with salt-
and-pepper-colored hair that was cut short and neat. He wore a wide-
sleeved, heavy tunic that covered his arms, the odd garment
appearing to be spun of golden thread. She narrowed her eyes at the
embroidered bands of geometric patterns that ran from his shoulders

to the hem, feeling like she had seen something similar not so long ago. "Who in the name of Olodumare are you? What have you done?" she asked, eyeing the droplets of rain as she rose to her feet, cautiously backing away from him.

"Greetings, Vesper of the Ose," he said in a formal tone, offering his hand. "I am guardian Shoyebi of the Nok. As to what I've done... well, it's difficult to explain. But let's just say I've cut out a few moments of time so that I may repair the damage you and that savage have done, before it's too late."

Vesper eyed his hand as if it were a snake, "How do you know me?"

Guardian Shoyebi held his hand out for a moment longer before letting it fall to its side, his face twisting with a sour look. "You may not know me, but I have known you for your entire life," he began. "You are chosen, like my ward and student, whom you met a few days ago."

Vesper immediately formed a gladius when a familiar young man appeared from a shimmering portal behind Shoyebi, her attention pulled to the geometric patterns of Ase that were bright against the dark skin on his arms. "I remember him, Seye, seeker of Ogun," she said, her thoughts going back to their battle with him in the alley only days ago. "He called me a thief. He tried to kill me—and failed."

The young man gritted his teeth, his nostrils flaring as he surged forward, only to be stopped by Guardian Shoyebi putting a hand to his chest. "She refused to—"

"Silence!" said Shoyebi, glaring over his shoulder. "You have caused enough trouble with your foolish behavior."

"I don't have time for this," she snapped, her attention focused on Narcissus. "I don't care who you are or what you want. I have a life to save, so either help me, or get out of my sight, and stop wasting my time."

Shoyebi smiled at her, raising an eyebrow. "Magda said you were willful and stubborn."

The mention of her aunt sent a chill through her, shaking loose a memory from long ago. "It was you," said Vesper, pressing her lips together. "That night in the garden. The night Magda died! She was speaking to you somehow; you spoke of other children, other chosen."

"You have a good memory," he said, nodding to her. "And now we have come full circle."

"I don't understand," she said, cocking her head.

"You have been left on your own for too long," began Shoyebi, taking on a lecturing tone. "With Magda dead, it falls to me to be your guardian. To continue your training, before it's too late."

Vesper scoffed at him, shaking her head. "Too late? No, I'm afraid you're the one who is too late. Olodumare knows I have much to learn, but I know enough to get by. I have responsibilities that I cannot just cast aside," she said, her voice dropping as she finished.

"These parlor tricks were meant to frighten the weak minded," he said, turning his eyes to the storm while waving a hand dismissively.

"It was enough to beat your student," she said, pressing her lips together, regretting the words the moment they left her mouth. "Apologies. That was unkind. Magda raised me better than that."

"Do not apologize for being right," he said, looking over his shoulder to his ward. "Magda said you had unnatural strength. And after years under my tutelage, Seye should have bested you with ease, but that was not the case."

"Gratitude, but none of this matters. The life of someone I care about hangs in the balance. Nothing matters more to me at this moment than saving him."

"Seye," snapped the older man, pointing to Narcissus. "Show me that you have understood the lessons. Do what must be done to save her man."

"You would waste our strength on this?" growled Seye, pushing past his guardian with a sneer on his face. "On her Roman dog!"

"Just do as I say, prove to me that you deserve my teachings, that I have not wasted my time with you."

Vesper's hand twitched as she held back the urge to throttle him. Instead, she took a deep breath and held her tongue. If this Seye could save Narcissus, she would bear his arrogance. "The wound is deep, through his back," she said softly. "And he is a Celt, not a Roman."

"Is that supposed to make it better?" said Seye, wrinkling his nose while he probed the wound with his fingers. "At least the Romans bathe."

"Can you save him?" she snapped, bristling at the insult.

Seye shrugged, closing his eyes while bowing his head. Curious as to what he was doing, Vesper shifted her vision to the world beyond, raising an eyebrow when she saw that an enormous amount of Ase flowed from the markings on his arms, and she pursed her lips in surprise when she finally caught a glimpse of the baobab under his brown leather vest, watching in fascination while it pulsed and flickered. "What have you done here?" He gasped suddenly, looking up at her, eyes filled with wonder.

"You mean the bond?" asked Vesper, making a sour face while he probed her connection with Narcissus, feeling violated, like he was touching her soul.

"Yes," he said, nodding to himself. "How is such a thing possible?"

Vesper hugged herself, a chill running through her while he delved deeper. "I don't remember," she said. "He was near death, and I had joined with a loa, sharing its knowledge."

"You despoil yourself!" he said, looking down his nose at her. "Taking on such corruption. It is beyond vulgar."

Shoyebi tapped his ward on the shoulder, clucking his tongue. "Do not pass judgment without knowing another's struggles. You have had the privilege of spending your days sheltered from the world, while Vesper has been forced to live in it."

"Apologies, Guardian," said Seye. "I will try to do better."

"Your apology should be directed, not to me, but to her."

Seye's nostrils flared as he offered her a tight-lipped smile. "Apologies."

"Just help him," she said, not caring for his forced words.

"I will try," he said, eyeing her up and down, "but I dare not use my reserves. Instead, I will use this bizarre connection you have to transfer Ase from you to him, using your strength to stitch his wounds. Do you understand?"

Vesper pressed her lips together, shaking her head. "No... but if it saves him, I will do what I must."

Seye shrugged once more, bowing his head in concentration as the geometric patterns on his arms cast them all in a warm glow. "This will feel... a little strange."

Vesper was about to ask how when suddenly, her stomach clenched, the breath in her lungs fleeing while she fought to stay conscious. The pain in her belly spread up to her chest, and she fell on top of Narcissus, arching her back as if her innards were being pulled out. "It burns," she said through clenched teeth.

"It will be over soon," said Shoyebi, looking down at her with a blank expression on his face as if they were discussing the weather. "Pain is a part of life, a lesson that you must learn to endure, a lesson that I will teach you."

She nodded as beads of sweat rolled down her temples, the heat burning through her body growing with each passing moment. Vesper's eyes snapped open wide when Seye pulled the spear from Narcissus and threw it aside, the sensation in her belly changing, her skin growing clammy and cold as her eyes grew heavy, "What are you doing?" she managed as she lost all sensation, her entire body numb. "I can't... I can't feel him."

A hint of a smile crossed Seye's face, and Vesper screamed when something inside her snapped, the gut-wrenching agony making her see spots at the edge of her vision. "You are whole again," he said simply, "and so is he."

Sensation returned, and Vesper could feel Narcissus was warm to the touch, his chest rising and falling with a steady rhythm, but nothing more. She could not feel anything beyond her senses. "What did you do?" she snapped, reaching out to grab Seye by his brown tunic, but failing when her hand fell limp at her side.

"We did what you asked," said Shoyebi, picking at a piece of lint on his fine tunic. "Now we must go, before we do any more damage to this foul place."

Vesper managed to shake her head, her voice little more than a croak. "No... please, I can't just leave him."

The guardian bowed his head, pressing his lips together. "Along the path of every chosen, there comes a time when they must make a choice to leave childish pursuits in the past," he said, looking down his nose at her. "That time is upon you now, Vesper. If you wish to learn the limits of your power, to learn the history of your people and how you may shape the future, you must come with us."

Looking back at Narcissus, she could see hints of pink on his pale features, while his breathing was steady as his massive chest rose and fell. "Can he come?"

Shoyebi shook his head, frowning at the massive Celt. "Where we go is not a place for outsiders, but if you wish, you can remain here in ignorance, and live out your life as a failed djambe with your destiny and duty forgotten, while the world falls to darkness."

Vesper stiffened as if he'd slapped her. From a young age, her parents, then her aunt had instilled a profound sense of duty in her. It was why she chose to stay in Rome when she could have fled long ago. Why she fought against the Sandawei, even while Commodus hunted for her and Narcissus, and why she had to make the decision she made now. "I will come with you," she said, swallowing hard as the words fell from her lips.

Without another word, Seye waved his hand, and a rippling pool appeared in front of them, waving and bending like waves on the ocean. "He will survive," he said, waving her through the portal, "and one day, you may fight at his side once more, but for now... destiny calls."

Vesper clutched at her belly, feeling hollow, missing the connection she shared with him. "I will be back. I promise," she whispered, taking one last look at him as she stepped through the portal, leaving Rome, and the man she loved, far behind.

THIRTEEN
FALLEN KINGS

Lucilla lurched toward the cave opening on legs that shook like a newborn foal. Her back, knees, and hands aching in protest from her relentless climb. When she had reached the top of the plateau and saw the flickering orange glow coming from the cave, she dismissed it as her exhausted mind playing tricks on her, but when the smell of roasting meat reached her nose, making her mouth water, she somehow found the strength to stagger to her feet, approach the cave with a mix of gut-clenching worry, and ravenous hunger.

Unsure of what else to do, she crouched low, making as little noise as she could, cursing when her stomach betrayed her, growling like a beast.

"There be no point in sneaking, woman," said a voice, speaking in a familiar, halting cadence that made Lucilla stop short, covering her mouth to stifle a scream. "Ya already yelled loud enough for all the damned to hear!"

Lucilla froze in place, feeling stupid for doing so. "Are you real? Or are you damned? Like everything else in this horrid place?"

"I be damned for sure," said the voice, full of amusement. "But be assured, I be as real as you. Come, come, fill your belly before its rumble call down the mountain."

Lucilla let out a breath she didn't know she was holding and peeked into the cave, raising an eyebrow when she found a dark-skinned man sitting cross-legged, his milky-white gaze going wide with shock for an instant when he saw her. "You are Sandawei," she said, taking a step back, her lips pressing together as she eyed the familiar markings and chalky-white paint covering his dark skin.

"And despite bearing the markings of my people, you be a Roman," he countered, unfolding his long legs and standing to tower over her, the bones tied to the side of his head clicking together when he bowed ever so slightly in way of a greeting. "But I won't hold it against you How do you come to be here?"

Lucilla frowned at the markings on his arms that matched her own, craning her neck to look him in the eye. He was bone thin, being easily the tallest man she had ever seen, and despite his claims that he was alive, he was little more than skin and bone, his face gaunt and hollow. "It is a long story." she said, returning his greeting with a nod of her own.

The tall Sandawei continued to stare, frowning at her arms. "If you be here, a long story it is for certain," he said, returning to his seat by the fire, folding his impossibly long legs beneath him, his attention locked on a meat-filled spit that he slowly turned over a bed of hot coals. "Not many make it this high, the last jump. It not be for the timid."

Lucilla opened her mouth to speak, but her belly protested, growling like a wild animal when a whiff of smoky, roasted flesh filled her nostrils. "Apologies," she said, her pale skin flushing a bright shade of pink in embarrassment.

"Do not apologize for hunger," he said, motioning for her to sit. "My stomach often rules me, and I have been so long without company, I forget my manners. Come, come, share my supper. Tell me how you have come to be wandering among the damned, in this place even Olodumare has forgotten."

She was taken aback by his courtesy, and after a moment's hesitation, she folded her legs beneath her and sat, grateful for the warmth of the fire. "Apologies. You are nothing like the Sandawei I have met."

"I be Papa Keita, Ọba to the Sandawei people. It is clear by your *itan* that you have spent time among my people. I am curious how this be; we are not fond of outsiders."

"Itan? You mean these?" asked Lucilla, realizing that his milky eyes were focused on the cuts Magnus had carved on her arms. "It was not by choice."

He nodded. "That makes sense," he said, tearing off a sizzling piece of meat from the spit and offering it to her. "Long ago, the itan were meant to tell the world who you are, your father, mother, brothers, and sisters, what you Romans would call history, but those are not like any I have seen with these old eyes. They symbolize power, strength. But more, they remove what is already there, preparing the body for something else."

"I have seen the ritual to completion. I know what they are meant for," said Lucilla, pushing away the memory of all the poor senator's that mother Ayaba stabbed in the chest. With a sigh, she took the charred meat, hot grease rolling down her fingers and burning the roof of her mouth as she devoured the delectable roast. "Rabbit?" she asked, licking her fingers with glee.

"Rat," he said simply, tearing a piece off for himself and swallowing it whole.

She stopped mid-chew, wrinkling her nose in disgust, wondering how rats could live in such a place, and what they ate to grow so big. She was once empress of Rome, the most powerful woman in the world, and now she found herself in a cave on the edge of nowhere, eating rats, of all things. She was about to put it aside when her stomach rumbled once more, and she remembered her months in her cell beneath the Colosseum, eating nothing but tasteless puls. "Hunger makes the best sauce," she said with a shrug, taking another bite, closing her eyes while enjoying the smoky flavor.

"You be wise," he said with an approving nod. "Now, tell me,

who you be? How do you possess these markings? How did you come
to this place?"

Lucilla wiped her grease-covered lips on her shoulder, all sense of
decorum forgotten as she took another bite. She cocked her head, re-
tracing the decisions that had brought her to this place. The burden
of responsibility had always been the bane of her existence, the need
to sacrifice her place in life. Always pushed into the difficult path,
while those around her were blessed with power and rank. Her father
had chosen Commodus over her to rule Rome despite his obvious
madness. Her first husband had chosen war over her. She was always
what Saoterus had once called her, a pretty bauble traded between
those more powerful than her. She decided that it would not happen
again; she would forge a different path. "Apologies. You are very kind,
but I made a promise to myself not long ago," she said, raising her
chin. "I will tell you what you wish to know, but you will go first.
How did you come to be here, and despite your kindness, why should
I trust a man like you?"

"I have shared my fire, my food. I have asked for nothing in
return."

"Yes," she said, looking around the cave, "but your people are
enemies of Rome, have killed innocent Romans. You live among the
damned, unhurt, unbroken, you understand my concern."

Papa Keita fell silent, his milky eyes never leaving hers. After
what felt like an eternity, he nodded, spreading his arms wide. "Very
well, I will show you who I am. Come, come," he said. Unfolding his
lanky body, he rose, motioning for her to follow as he walked deeper
into the cave. Raising an open palm to his face, he blew a soft breath
over his hand. Lucilla blinked when the tips of his long fingers began
to glow with a cold white light, casting flickering shadows on the
walls, revealing a vast fresco covering every inch of the cave. "It will
change little... and I will be proud to tell you my story."

"What's all this?" she asked.

"Look, look, this is my tapestry. How the world saw me during
my time," he said in a hushed tone, pointing to a crude drawing of

green hills and a series of small towns, all of them growing together under the shelter of an eagle's outspread wings. "When I first drew breath in the world, this was Rome. Little more than a few outgrown villages, huddled together for safety around the seven hills."

Lucilla narrowed her eyes at the image, recognizing hints of the city she knew today. "Impossible," she said, looking him up and down, noting that he was fit and healthy despite the wrinkles on his gaunt face. "That was centuries ago."

Papa Keita ignored her statement, his long stride taking them deeper into the cave. "You Romans always thought highly of yourselves, molding the world in your image, calling yourselves a republic even when you were little more than barbarian kings who stole even your gods from others."

"What does that have to do with you?" said Lucilla through gritted teeth, the insult to the city of her birth driving her to anger.

"Because I am the one who did not see your threat. I am the one who let your corruption spread beyond these seven hills."

He pointed to another image, an image of a tall man with dark skin with a crown of golden bones dangling from the side of his head. "Is that supposed to be you?" she asked, her curiosity growing.

"Yes. In the language of my people, Ọba is a king, ruler of all."

Lucilla scoffed, shaking her head. "Your people have never ruled, not in the most distant of histories. From what I understand this was a punishment for your arrogance and cruelty, punishment from the great god Olodumare."

The tall man's eyes narrowed, and he gave her a strange look. "History is written by the conquerors. Trust me when I say, we Sandawei held the world in our thrall," he said nodding to himself. "Now, tell me, how do you know the history of my people?"

She was about to speak of Vesper, of her father, and the truth she had discovered about the Sandawei, of what she knew of the Ose, but then she continued to stare at the tapestry of his life. There was more to the story than he was telling her. Her eyes were drawn to images just at the edge of the light, images of war, conquest, and blood, pictures that told stories of a harsh rule filled with decadence and depravity. Their eyes met, and she saw that these parts of the story were true as well, and her hackles rose, trust vanishing, replaced by worry. "One of my teachers, he was from Africa Proconsularis," she said, the lie coming easy to her lips."He knew of the Ose... and their enemies, the Sandawei."

His face twisted to an ugly frown at the mention of Vesper's people, the Ose. "Traitors," he spat, moving on to point to an image of a mob of dark-skinned warriors surrounding the king, their spears raised for violence. "Over the centuries, we had grown complacent, secure in our power, but it was I who ignored the growing danger of Rome, not seeing until it was too late."

"They cast you out," said Lucilla, following his milky eyes to a new image, that of a woman with caramel-colored skin, with her arms above her head, opening a shimmering portal. "Who is that!?"

"The Usurper," he said through clenched teeth. "She did not have the power to grant me the final death. I was too strong. Instead, she convinced the people that I was not fit to rule, that my sight had failed me, and that the Sandawei would be destroyed if they spent too long in the shadow of Rome."

"Mother Ayaba," whispered Lucilla, gooseflesh running up and down her arms the longer she looked at the crude painting.

Beside her, Papa Keita cursed, his words so vile, that it made her ears burn. "You know her!" he said, slamming his fist against the wall, smearing blood from his fist across the image of the Sandawei matron.

"Yes," she said, leaping back, worried that, in his rage, he would hurt her.

"Do not fear me," he said, reading her thoughts. "The rage is natural. You speak the name of my greatest enemy, that you have been delivered to me. It is a sign of Olodumare's hand guiding events."

Ignoring him, Lucilla backpedaled, never taking her eyes from him. "She is part of the reason I am here," she said, almost tripping over a basket filled with chalk and pots of colored paint. "I fled from her and her ward, a Sandawei posing as a Roman."

"Yes, yes, that was always her way, attacking from the shadows, invisible until the moment she strikes. She fooled me the same way, turning those I trusted against me," he said, stalking toward her with a hungry look in his eyes. "But you know her, have been in her presence?"

Lucilla licked her lips, taking a quick glance over her shoulder to the cave entrance, wondering how far she could get from him if she ran. "It cannot be the same woman. That would make her centuries old, the both of you."

"We Sandawei are masters of death," he said, suddenly on top of her, his massive hands gripping her shoulders. "Time is nothing to us."

"You're hurting me," she said, twisting and turning to break his iron grip.

Papa Keita snapped his hands open, taking a step away from her. "I beg your forgiveness," he said, his skinny body shaking. "The enemy of my enemy is my ally. I would never harm a hair on your head."

"No, no, I want no part in this," she said. "I've already paid the price for my involvement. Look at me, I've lost everything except my life. I don't—"

The tall man shook his head, waving her off. "You don't understand. The risk would be mine and mine alone."

"How so?" she said, raising her chin high.

Papa Keita bounced on his heels, his long fingers brushing against the markings on her arms. "You must understand, the itan on your arms. The ritual be not complete. You be an open door."

Lucilla gripped her stomach, sucking in deep breaths to calm her nerves. She had suspected that Mother Ayaba was doing such things, that the senators, while they looked like themselves, were different men, their souls replaced by the ritual and a final thrust of the matron's dagger. "I will not let you take my soul" she said. "I will not—"

"I propose no such thing," he said, shaking his head frantically, setting the bones tied to the side of his head to a mad clatter. "We will be equals. Allies."

"Allies... in what?"

"Vengeance," he rasped, starting to pace, bowing his head while muttering under his breath.

Lucilla raised a fine eyebrow, her eyes drawn to the fresco covering the cave walls. If his story were true, he was someone important, someone powerful who could stand against the matron. "She has used the ritual on half the Roman Senate."

Papa Keita stopped, narrowing his milky gaze on her. "How? It is not an easy thing; the subject of the ritual must be calm, at ease."

"It is my fault. I led her to them," she said, her mouth going dry. "They opened their doors, and welcomed us into their homes because I was with her."

"You are not just some bored patrician woman playing with forces she does not know? You are someone with enough position that Rome's powerful will open the door when you come calling?"

Lucilla nodded, cursing herself for her weakness, for letting Magnus take her from her cell, for agreeing to help Mother Ayaba without truly seeing the danger she represented. "I am Annia Aurelia Galeria Lucilla," she said, letting her arms fall to her sides while standing proudly. "Daughter to Marcus Aurelius, wife to Lucius Aurelius Verus, and sister to Commodus, all emperors of Rome, past and present."

He sucked in a breath, his gaunt face creasing in a smile. "A powerful line, a powerful woman. We will do well together."

"That is the first time I have seen you smile," she said, returning to her seat by the fire, tearing off another rat from the spit and offering it to the tall man.

"We Sandawei are not an emotional people," he said, taking his seat and accepting the sizzling meat with a nod of his head. "It is said that this is why Olodumare replaced us with the fool Ose."

They ate in silence for a time, the only sound being the occasional pop and sizzle from the rats on the spit. Finally, when her stomach had quieted, Lucilla gave him a hard look. "What must I do?"

Papa Keita put down his food, resting his arms on his knees, "I am trapped here, my flesh will never again leave this place." he said, his eyes never blinking, "But my spirit...In the right vessel,"

"You mean me."

"Yes, we will be allies in every sense of the world, two souls in one body. You will have all my power, my wisdom. My hunger for revenge."

Lucilla looked down at her bloodied hands and knees, knowing how she got here. She had been spurned for ambitions, but now, she had found her path to power, true power, not that given to her by someone else, "You will have my hunger for revenge as well. My ambition"

"Yes. I will know what you know, desire what you desire, and you will have the same from me."

"Well then," she said, clenching her hands into fists, her nostrils flaring. "Shall we begin?"

FOURTEEN
COLD IRON

"Wake up, dog, or I promise, I'll put another javelin in your belly!"

Narcissus sputtered awake, choking from ice cold water splashed in his face, his heartbeat thundering in his ears. His first impulse was to clutch at the spear in his belly, expecting pain and blood, only to find himself straining against iron shackles, his pale face reddening from the failed effort. "What is the meaning of this," he growled, blinking away the water in his eyes as he came fully awake. Looking around, he was surprised to find not the arena, but a deep, dank cell with his arms shackled to a rough-hewn stone wall, men and women chained alongside him, while the only light came from a small, barred window high above him. Glancing down to his stomach, he shook his head in confusion when he found his leather armor gone. Stranger still, where he expected to have a hole in his stomach there was nothing. He was whole, with only his pink flesh under his shag of red hair.

He was about to speak to the woman chained to the wall beside him when his head snapped forward by someone grabbing him by the scruff of his beard. He found himself face-to-face with a Praetorian guardsmen, wearing their typical black leather armor and purple cloak, leaning in close enough that he could smell the man's stale breath of cheap wine and too much garlic. "Eyes forward, beast."

"Let go of me," he said in a low voice full of menace, sucking in a deep breath and pulling on the shackles with all his might, "or I will snap your puny neck."

The man let go, snorting at him before turning to face another Praetorian with a purple sash of office running from shoulder to hip over his armor. "Prefect, he is awake."

The prefect came into view, flanked by another guardsman. In the dim light, Narcissus could just make him out, taking note of his cleft chin, swarthy skin, and piercing green eyes that never seemed to blink. "I know you," said Narcissus. "The emperor's chamber boy...Cleander. Have you fallen so low that he now sends you to deal with escaped slaves and convicts, or have you been cast out by that madman, replaced by another, with more brains and skill."

"You are brave for a man who is about to die by my blade," said Cleander, fingering the ornate gladius at his hip.

"Then do it," said Narcissus, straining once more against the iron shackles. "I have no fear of death, do you?" With a roar, the big Celt snapped forward, testing the metal to its limits. He showed them a feral grin, and in unison, all three men jumped back, the one who had grabbed his beard falling onto his bottom.

Cursing, Cleander dragged the fallen Praetorian guardsmen to his feet, his face a mask of twisting rage. "Watch him," he snapped, holding the hilt of his gladius in a white-knuckled grip. "I have orders to tell him when the Celt has awoken. I shall return soon."

"Coward," shouted Narcissus, deep-throated laughter pouring from his throat when Cleander said nothing, leaving in a huff through a heavy wooden door, while the remaining Praetorians took a few tentative steps back, their eyes never leaving him. With the immediate threat gone, he leaned back against the wall and closed his eyes, his mind going to those last few minutes in the Colosseum. He could clearly remember throwing the javelin at Commodus, remembered him falling from sight, only for him to reappear a heartbeat later with an ugly gash on his side. After that, the rest was a blur. There were flashes of pain and blood from his belly. Vesper leaning over him, her beautiful face full of worry—then nothing. At the thought of Vesper, he gasped, his body tingling with shock. "She's gone," he whispered, a hollow feeling forming in his chest.

"Quiet," said the Praetorian who had grabbed him by the beard, "or—"

"Or what? You'll fall on your bottom again?" he mocked.

The man snapped his mouth shut while his partner's shoulders shook with repressed laughter. "Or I'll gut you like the pig you are," he countered, pulling his gladius halfway out of his sheath.

Narcissus spat, knowing an empty threat when he heard one. Cleander told them to watch him, not kill, which meant that the emperor's errand boy went to fetch someone. He searched his memoires once more, shaking his head when he could not recall anything about what happened after he fell. He had no clue if anyone had gotten away or even if they still lived. "You, there, Praetorian," he called out. "What happened to the woman I was with?"

The guardsman who had woken him sneered, striding toward him. "I told you to silence that foul tongue," he said, grabbing him by the beard once more. "But if you must know, most of them are dead. Commodus was kind enough to reward us with a few of the slave women. Darius and I made out better than most, getting the clean ones, doing what we willed until they were spent. After we were done, my blade made easy work of them."

At the thought of this vile man laying with Vesper, then killing her, Narcissus saw red, his blood burning with rage. The Praetorian's eyes went wide with shock when the big Celt clipped him with his fist, his adrenaline-fueled haymaker tearing the iron shackle clean off the wall. Clutching at his bruised jaw, he fought to pull away, but Narcissus was quicker, catching him by the throat with a massive hand before he could move. "I told you! If you touched me again, I would snap your neck!" The hapless Praetorian clawed at his hand, but Narcissus felt no pain, instead pulling him in close, twisting his neck with both hands until it snapped, a horrid gurgle echoing throughout the cell.

The other guardsmen watched the body fall in wide-eyed horror, unsheathing his gladius and holding it out in front of him. "The women... they died well," he began, shuffling back. "And I was kind to them, only using them for my pleasure. Cassius, he was the one who became vulgar, cutting them for sport."

The more the man spoke, the deeper his rage grew, his nostrils flaring like a charging bull. Using both hands, and planting his foot against the rough-hewn brick, Narcissus tore the remaining shackle from the wall, stalking toward the other Praetorian guardsmen while the iron dragged and clanged against the concrete floor. "You will pay for every death tenfold," he said through clenched teeth.

The Praetorian turned to run, bolting for the door, only to stumble face-first onto the floor when Narcissus clipped him in the back of the head with his iron shackle. The big Celt was on top of him in the span of a single breath, wrapping the chains around the man's neck, pulling so hard that the veins on his muscled arms bulged, "The bodies!" he seethed, spittle running down his beard. "What did you do with them?"

"P-pyre," he said, trying to pry the big Celt's hands from the chain. "B-burned, all burned."

Narcissus did not remember snapping the man's neck or even how long he sat there on his back, his arms bulging as he strained to pull the chains ever tighter, piling all of his rage on the dead man's broken body. He only remembered the voice that brought him back to his senses, the voice of a man who had been at his side for more years than he could remember.

"Doctore? Are you well?"

He blinked, his arms shaking as he let go of the chains. "Linus? How are you here?" he said, looking up to see his friend's wrinkled face, his eyes full of worry.

The old gladiator opened his mouth to speak, only to snap his mouth shut when his body was jerked back, Narcissus seeing at last that his old friend wore a chain around his neck, and that they were not alone. "He is here because we wish it."

"Commodus!?" barked Narcissus, his instincts taking over as he rolled off the dead man and onto his feet, hefting the corpse up in front of him like a shield.

The emperor threw back his head, his eerie laughter echoing off the rough-hewn walls. "Dead men make for poor shields. Living ones, they work best," he said, shaking Linus to make his point.

They stared at each other for a moment, Commodus giving him an expectant look. Narcissus let the dead Praetorian fall at his feet. "You ruin your reputation, Linus. Keeping company with the worst Rome has to offer."

"Apologies, Doctore," said the old gladiator. "This is the best I could find at the brothel."

"That's what happens when you spend time with the lowest of the low," said Narcissus.

Linus began to laugh, only to fall silent Commodus put a knee into his bent back while pulling at his chain, bending the old man over backward. "Apologies, Caesar," he gasped, his bronzed face going pale.

"Enough," shouted Narcissus, letting his hands fall to his sides. "What in the name of the gods do you want?"

Commodus pushed Linus to the floor and then handed the chain to Cleander, who appeared behind him. "We spent the afternoon thinking of how to kill you, Celt," he said, stepping forward. "Can you imagine that. Caesar Commodus Augustus himself, ruler of the greatest empire in the history of mankind, wasting thoughts on a lowly slave."

Narcissus looked Commodus up and down, looking for weakness. A weak side, or a limp, but found nothing. He was powerfully built, a giant of a man, one of the few who could look Narcissus in the eye without craning their neck. "What have you decided?" he said, standing his ground as the emperor came closer. "Something amusing, I hope. I always wanted a spectacular death. One that the people of Rome would speak to their children about."

"I went through the usual ones," said Commodus, coming to a halt, unbuttoning his tunic. "Lions would have been fun, or ravens plucking out your eyes. They can be trained to do that, far more intelligent than most animals, not to mention some slaves. I even thought of having you cooked, serving you at a feast in our honor—cooked Celt; it would have been amusing."

"Sounds common, even boring," said Narcissus, swallowing hard while adjusting his stance. He had fought Commodus in the arena months ago during their escape. He was strong, stronger than him, but he was still a man, the javelin in his belly had proved that. "Why not give me a games to remember: Narcissus against the best gladiators in the empire. The crowds would love it."

Commodus looked back at Linus, then to Cleander, and Narcissus tensed, ready to pounce. "We tried that," he said, looking back at him. "You and your friends embarrassed me by not dying as planned. In fact, it has been three times now that you have defied me."

Narcissus stuck out his chest, nodding to himself. He was about to die; he was sure of it. Commodus was done with his games and would simply do away with him in this dark, dank cell, forgotten by the world. "Do it, then. Kill me and be done with it, or are you going to let your errand boy do it for you?"

"And that, my dear Cleander, is why we are a god among men," he said, winking back at the swarthy prefect before returning his attention to Narcissus.

The big man narrowed his eyes, frowning into his beard. "What do you mean?"

Commodus spread his arms wide, gazing around the room. "Look around you; look at the strength you show," he said, pointing to the dead guardsmen. "Even chained to the wall, you managed to kill the men guarding you."

"The chains were weak," he grumbled, looking down at his hands. "As were your men."

"No, it's more than that," said Commodus. "In fact, you will live for a long time."

"I have tasted freedom, and I will never again submit to the life of a slave. You will have to kill me."

"Defiant to the end," said Commodus. "That's why we decided that we like you."

A choking sound escaped from Cleander, and Narcissus looked over to see the man's face red with rage. "Caesar! This man is dangerous, a leader of the slave rebellion. He cannot be allowed to live; he will draw others to his cause, try to escape!"

"Not if I have his friends, his woman," said Commodus, smiling like a cat with an animal trapped in its grip. "We will keep his woman, and his friend. Give them a life of comfort, and in return, you will serve us. Won't you?"

"Why would you do this?" said Narcissus, shaking his head. "Killing me, no matter how painful, would be easier, more satisfying?"

"No," he whispered, removing his tunic to show off his muscled physique, leaving him completely naked. "Having you at our side, doing our will... even teaching me."

Narcissus scoffed, frowning at a large gash on the emperor's flank. "Teach you what?"

"How you fight," he said, eyeing the gash. "Your Ose witch has done something to you. What, I cannot say. While you are not our equal, you are stronger, tougher than any man I have faced in battle, so you will serve me, protect me, and teach me your barbaric ways of battle."

Narcissus felt like he'd been kicked in the gut, his mouth going dry as every instinct told him to die trying to kill the foul man, but one look at Linus, the idea that he had Vesper alive somewhere stayed his hand. "I promised I would kill you," he said, his eyes drilling into the emperor's.

"A fine threat, but an empty one," said Commodus. "If I die, Cleander has orders to kill your friend here, then your woman. Not to mention he will have games, where a thousand women and children will be killed in your name. Do you understand?"

For the first time in his life, Narcissus was struck silent, opening and closing his mouth. He could not let Vesper, or Linus die, and he would not let the blood of innocents stain his hands. "Very well," he whispered after what felt like forever.

"I didn't hear you," said Commodus, taking back the chain that held Linus.

"I will serve!" shouted Narcissus, bowing his head. "You have my word."

"Good!" said Commodus, "I have had a feast prepared in your honor. I wish to show you off, so my men will take you to the baths, and get you cleaned up, shave off all that hair, the beard especially."

FIFTEEN
A LAST THREAD

Vesper had always traveled alone along the threads that bound together the tapestry of life, never with others. The experience was jarring, and she kept fighting for control, reaching for threads along the path only to find Seye's hand already firmly in place, forcing her to surrender to his control. To make matters worse, the longer they traveled along this filament, the fewer threads appeared, like the connecting lines were burning away, leaving only a single thread, vibrating alone in an empty void.

They emerged from the portal, and Vesper's lungs and nostrils burned, each breath an agony as she sucked in scalding hot air. "Where in Olodumare are we?" she gasped, squinting in a vain effort to see through the blinding light stinging her eyes.

Seye leaped ahead of them with an unsheathed blade, holding out in front of him, his eyes ever moving. Guardian Shoyebi emerged after her, the shimmering circle evaporating like rain on hot stone. "We call this place *eyi tio gbeyin asale*, the last oasis," he said, pulling back the sleeve of his wide tunic to reveal an arm that was heavily marked by the twisted, geometric patterns of the Nok, his people.

Vesper watched in fascination, not daring to blink, while he chanted in his strange tongue, spinning his arm in a way that made her dizzy. A moment later, one of the geometric patterns on his arm came to life, bending and stretching into a wide circle of thin verdant green that floated like a tree branch over their heads. "It is not much, but it will provide shade against the relentless sun."

Vesper's eyes finally adjusted under the shade, and she looked around to find nothing but rolling hills and wide planes of golden sand as far as the eye could see, with the oasis being nothing more than a pool of water no wider than a man was tall, surrounded by a few prickly plants. "You have a strange way of using Ase," she said, falling in beside the guardian as Seye started off.

"We have little choice. Ase is fading from the world; as such we do our best to conserve what we can," said Shoyebi, his tone blunt with little inflection.

"Fading? No, the weave in Rome is tattered, corrupt, but once out of the city... there is an abundance of..." Vesper's voice trailed away as they gained some distance from the oasis, her hand falling to her stomach when a wave of emptiness came over her as she looked out over the endless desert. "What's happened here? This isn't like the city with its tattered weave: it's worse, far worse."

"You begin to understand," said Shoyebi, giving her a sidelong glance. "Rome is sick, dying, but this, this is the final result of such corruption."

"There's nothing here," whispered Vesper, shivering despite the heat. "It's dead, no weave, no connections. No life. How do your people survive in such a desolate place?"

Seye turned back to face them fully, his lips turned down into an ugly frown. "We have adapted! Protected what is ours from outsiders, and when we can, take back the power stolen from us over the centuries."

"I told you I am no thief," began Vesper, meeting his accusing stare with one of her own.

"Enough, Seye, there are no threats here for now. You are not needed for my protection. Go ahead, tell the council that I have found Magda's ward and they should prepare," said the guardian, returning his attention to her when the seeker sped off, running at a breakneck pace despite the heat. "Apologies. He has spent most of his life defending our people from outsiders and has known too much loss for one so young. Now, come along, it's not much farther."

"Why live in such a desolate place?" she asked, the emptiness growing the deeper they traveled into the desert.

"You will see," he said, picking up the pace, his tone making it clear she should hold questions for later. "We are not far now."

Vesper hurried after him, following in silence across the hard-packed desert sand in the blistering heat, with only Shoyebi's umbraculum for shade, she began to question her decision. To follow the guardian and his ward, with little proof, was madness or at the very least foolish. She worried about Narcissus, praying that he was well, wishing she could let him know that she was safe. They were almost to the top of a small hill when her face broke into a smile, her worries forgotten as a thrill ran through her. "A baobab," she said in disbelief. It was still miles away, but even from this distance, the great tree towered so high it almost touched the heavens, its wide branches giving life and shade to a small town spread out among its massive roots. "I thought the one in our home village was the last one of that size."

Guardian Shoyebi offered her a pained smile, nodding his head. "The tree that Magda guarded *was* the last. The great baobabs, those that have existed since creation are no more, only the young ones exist today, small by comparison."

Vesper stopped, casting a sidelong glance at the older man. "I don't understand," she said, still in awe of the great tree in the distance.

The guardian bowed his head, pressing his lips together. "It is easier to show you. Come, please."

They came to the outskirts of the village, and Vesper's confusion grew the closer she came to the great baobab. It was only when they were close enough to fall under its shadow that she truly understood, her brow knitting together when she craned her neck upward. Its wide trunk was covered in rot, its bark moist and flaking away in many parts to reveal the vulnerable wood underneath, while its towering branches were leafless, bare and bent, little more than skeletal claws reaching for the heavens. At the heart of its wide trunk was the worst of it, a massive crack, an open wound that spanned from stem to stern. "By Olodumare, what happened... to all of it!"

Shoyebi dropped his arm, and the shelter protecting them from the sun vanished, Vesper's eyes shooting open in awe when the geometric pattern reappeared on his flesh. "This place, all of it was once a verdant garden. The great baobabs covered the landscape as far as the eye could see, providing shelter, water, and life for all who lived here in peace."

"You mean all of this... the desert... was green?"

The guardian nodded, waving to a few villagers in the distance that watched over a herd of skinny goats chewing on the few shoots of green that pushed out from the rocky soil. "The first people lived here, those descended directly from the primordial loa, the Orishas created by Olodumare to govern the universe."

Vesper swallowed hard, touching the pattern of stars running across her throat from one side of her collarbone to the other. "I've met one," she said.

Shoyebi nodded, his eyes drawn to the tattoo on her neck. "Yes, Eshu. We felt the connection, even here, far away from the weave. This is one of the reasons we sent Seye to find you."

"Then why did he attack me?" she asked.

"Seye is a blunt instrument," he said, shaking his head. "All his life, his duty as seeker was to find and punish those who have taken from us. When he was given orders to find you, he did it in the only way he knew how."

"And now that he knows the truth," began Vesper, watching a

group of farmers in the distance walking in front a tiller made of pure Ase, leaving deep grooves in the earth in preparation of planting

"You bested him," said the guardian, linking his hands together behind his back, "You, even untrained, did things that we could only dream of, wielded Ase in ways we know of only in our history. As such, he feels a great shame when he looks at you."

Vesper bit the inside of her cheek to stop herself from laughing, having felt the same, amazed at his use of Ase in ways she couldn't even imagine. "The same could be said of him. And, apologies, but are they all chosen?" she asked, pointing to a small group of women dressed in red robes, their arms heavily tattooed with the geometric patterns of the Nok. She watched as many of the symbols broke away, spinning and bending until they took on shapes of all kinds, some scooping up large pools of water and pouring over recently seeded fields, while others acted like scythe, sweeping across fields of tall wheat, harvesting the golden grain.

Shoyebi followed her gaze, cocking his head. "Yes... and no," he said, looking back at her. "Life is difficult here, and we have done things that might seem strange to you, in an attempt to survive."

"They are all using Ase," she said, eyeing the other people in the fields doing the most mundane tasks with the power.

"It has become our way," he began, putting up his hands. "You know almost nothing of what it means to be chosen, of what you are capable of, of our culture."

"Apologies," said Vesper, returning her attention to the women. "This is not what I expected."

The guardian nodded, patting her on the shoulder. "I can Imagine. The women are using Ase, but they are not chosen."

"I didn't think that was possible."

"We have much to teach you, but to make it clear. They have no Ase of their own, they do what they do with borrowed potential, borrowed power."

Vesper's brow shot up, and she gave him a questioning look. "That does not sound... natural."

"Why? This is Ase provided by the great baobab, nothing more."

Vesper bowed her head, pushing back memories of the horrible things she had seen in her travels in the worlds beyond. "The Sandawei, they do such things. Olodumare cut them off from the weave long ago, so now, to maintain their power, they draw on corrupt forces from the worlds beyond the living, from the dead themselves."

The guardian looked away, coughing into his hand. "We are not like that. We only concern ourselves with keeping our baobab safe. That this last bastion of the first people survives long enough to pass on our traditions and values."

She could only nod dumfounded as they left the farms and pastures on the outskirts and drove deeper to the heart of the village, fascinated by the amount of Ase being channeled all around her. The streets were laid out around the great tree like a wagon wheel. Everyone they passed seemed to have the Ase markings on their arms and legs, with many bearing heart runes of the great baobab on their chests, and despite this place being far from her home, she felt a sense of ease here, a familiarity that came with village life. If she closed her eyes, she could swear she was home; the smells, and sounds, even the tempo was like the place she grew up. Curious, Vesper shifted her gaze in an attempt to see the weave, the connections, and a smile creased her face when she saw that they existed here. Her eyes followed the glowing threads of amber that made up a tapestry all on its own, apart from the weave that connected the rest of humanity... an oasis in a vast desert. When at last her eyes fell on the great baobab, her smile faded, and she had to grab on to Shoyebi's arm when her legs gave way from the shock. "What have you done!" she gasped, her moment of weakness quickly replaced by gut-wrenching horror, disgust.

Shoyebi opened his mouth in protest but quickly fell silent when he saw the look in her eyes, understanding that she could see the truth. After what felt like an eternity, he cleared his throat, whispering in a strained voice, "Only the chosen can see the weave. I did not think you had been trained in this. Please tell no one; my people have no idea what we had to do to survive."

Vesper shook her head, her face a mask of confusion as she fell to her knees, feeling betrayed, empty, regretting her decision to come here, her mind raced as to how she could escape this nightmare.

SIXTEEN
VENGEANCE

Lucilla's hand shook as she held the dagger: her pale cheeks flushed as she gathered her courage.

"You must do it. Your body is young and powerful, yet you lack the wisdom to do what we hunger for. The skin I wear is spent, but my mind is strong. Together, we will have all we desire."

She nodded, not really listening. Papa Keita had explained it to her over and over, and while she had seen Mother Ayaba do it many times, she had never stabbed anyone except for her brother. "I will try," she said, licking her lips while raising the dagger above her head with both hands. She sat back on her haunches while the Sandawei vodun lay on his back in front of her, newly carved symbols on his chest still dripping with blood, waiting. "It be easy, Lucilla, like killing a pig."

The dagger almost fell from her hands when she bent in half, her body shaking with laughter. "What a fool I've been," she said, shaking her head. "I've never killed a pig... much less anything else."

"We all be fools sometimes," he said, sitting up, "but it only matters that we one day wake up, leave foolish things in the past."

"But—"

"Do not let doubt consume you; vengeance is at hand," said Papa Keita, plucking the dagger from her hands, holding the tip of the weapon to his breastbone. "End this body; free my soul to join you. Together, we will rain down a fury the likes the world has never seen."

"You make it sound so easy."

With a growl, he took her hand in his, holding the weapon together around the leather-wrapped hit, squeezing hard. "It is! Take the blade. Say the words I have taught you! Put it in my chest!"

Lucilla sucked in a deep breath, gripping the dagger with all her strength. "Very well, lie back. I will do what must be done."

"Good!"

He returned to his back, and Lucilla raised the dagger over her head with both hands, repeating in her mind the words Papa Keita had given her. Shouting the words in the strange tongue, she closed her eyes, bringing the dagger down with all her might. A terrible scream filled her ears as the dagger twisted out of her hands, clattering away. Her eyes snapped open to find the vodun cursing in pain, clutching at his side, the blade having glanced off his bony rib cage. "Apologies," she shouted, while her hands shook with panic.

"Keep... your... eyes... open," he groaned, grabbing the dagger from where it fell, putting it once more in her hand. "I have no desire to die from a thousand cuts."

Lucilla grit her teeth, her eyes flashing with anger at the vodun. "I told you. I have never killed."

"Then it is past time you learned because our path to power will be bloody," he spat, lying back once more, his eyes never leaving hers. "This time, keep your eyes open."

"I will!" she said, her nostrils flaring. Lucilla let her anger take hold, her eyes never leaving the skinny man's breastbone. With a shout she thrust the blade down with all her might, gawking in disgust when it punctured his chest with a nauseating pop, halting only when the leather hilt blocked it from going deeper. She had expected blood, even a scream, but when the burning rush flowed up her arms, her heart stopped, and she found her hands locked in place on the leather-wrapped hilt. She opened her mouth to scream, but nothing came, with only a whimper escaping her throat as the heat climbed, rising from her arms into her chest, descending down to her pelvis. Feeling like her skin was burning, flesh bubbling and sizzling, like rats turning over on a spit.

It was over as quickly as it began, and Lucilla came back to her senses, hunched over Papa Keita's spent body, somehow looking more emaciated than he had in life, an aged skeletal husk despite him having been alive and breathing only moments before. Remembering the burning up and down her skin, she patted down her flesh in a rush, blinking in surprise when she found herself whole, with the markings on her arms and chest hardly visible.

"You be with me," said a voice in her head, sending her scrambling back to the cave wall just as she had calmed her racing heart, her stomach once again turning in knots.

"No! No! This was a mistake," she screeched, clutching the sides of her head while kicking her feet, feeling like something was crawling around under her skin. "Get out! Get out!"

The voice fell to a whisper, muttering words so low she was forced to stop and listen. "Do not fight; let the joining happen." The calm tone soothed her, slowed her racing heart. When memories of days she had never lived began to run through her mind, understanding dawned, her worry fading away like morning mist. She had feared losing herself, drowning in Papa Keita, with his mind taking over her own. Instead, she was simply more. She was still Lucilla, daughter of Marcus Aurelius, wife to Lucius Verus, and proud citizen of the greatest empire the world had ever known. Now, she was also Keita, vodun and oracle of the Sandawei. A king who had lived many lives in many bodies, a proud conqueror who had risen to great heights, only to be betrayed by the person he trusted the most, cast out by his own people to live in exile among the damned.

"This is wonderful," said Lucilla, all of her doubt and worry fading away, laughing in wonder as she stood, holding out her hands in front of her while flexing her fingers. "I feel like I could tear down the mountain... slay every shade!"

In her mind, the vodun adjusted, shifting and stretching as if two people were trying to wear the same stola, one which was far too small. "We will do much more," he said at last, the disjointed confusion fading as if they had always been like this.

"Then let us begin," she said through clenched teeth, her hunger for revenge growing with each passing moment. Raising her chin, Lucilla left the cave where Papa Keita had made his home since before she was born. Where the imprisoned vodun had hunted for rats, living deep in the bowels of the mountain, spent his endless days drawing out the tapestry of his life on the cave wall, dreaming of the vengeance which was now within their grasp.

Striding like an empress to the edge of her perch, Lucilla peered into the darkness, catching sight of the hordes of shades each time lightning brightened the sky, "The itan... the markings on my arms, they are what protected me before, will they again?"

"You know the answer. You know all the answers," he said. "It is all in you now."

Lightning flashed above her once more, and Lucilla raised her arms, secure in the understanding that she was protected from the dead, sure that she could not just hold them at bay, but do more, much more. Filling her lungs, she shouted out over the barren planes, her voice booming louder than thunder, "Mother Abaya, Senator Magnus, I come for you." She leapt from the cliff with a small smile across her face, relishing in the wind rushing past her, howling in her ear.

She landed in a titanic crash, stone and ash exploding all around her in a hail of destruction. She emerged from the crater unharmed to find the dead waiting for her, their cold dead hands reaching for a taste of life. Instead of shrinking away or running, she took them, wrenching them closer in a lovers' embrace. The dead wailed when she touched them, the itan on her arms flashing blue and white and spreading over their withered forms, turning them to dust. "It's glorious," said Lucilla, shuddering as she tore at them, consuming them. Each time closing her wounds, driving away fatigue, making her stronger.

"Control yourself," whispered Papa Keita, his voice growing more frantic each time she embraced a shade. "Lest we squander our true power."

Lucilla spun in a circle, her voice a mad cackle when the shades ran from her. "Why? The dead fear me," she spat. "Just as the matron and Magnus shall!"

"The dead will serve you, so use them, not only for our strength, but as an army that will shake the foundations of the universe."

"Then we shall!" At the vodun's urging, they set off across the vast plain to their destination, her back straight and her head held high, heart and soul bent on destruction. At first, each time a shade crossed her path, she consumed it, adding the dead to her strength, but after a time she followed Papa Keita's advice, binding them to her will by breaking their fragile minds until they knew only to obey her and nothing else. When, at last, they found the cobblestone path that crossed the world in between, Lucilla had amassed an army that spread out as far as the eye could see, spread out over the hills in both directions and beyond, the wailing of the dead drowning out all other sounds. "How do we find them?" she asked, not finding that knowledge in the vodun's thoughts. "Where are they hiding!"

Papa Keita delved into their memories, hunting, searching for the answer, gasping when they found it. "They have built a construct," he rasped. His words coming quick, Lucilla's blood racing, their desire for revenge making her blood boil.

At first she didn't understand, but a moment later, the knowledge was there, the intricate details of the world in between. With enough power, one could carve an offshoot of the cobblestone path, building a refuge atop the bones of the dead. "The lives required to build such a thing... it's beyond comprehension," said Lucilla. "How could anyone be so cruel."

"She has made bargains with the loa that the great god Olodumare banished long ago, before the age of the Sandawei. Loa that require payment in death and destruction for the boons they grant."

"Can we defeat her?" she asked, stumbling while putting a hand to her chest, her brow creased with worry.

In her mind, the vodun fell silent, her feelings of dread amplified by his own. "Apart, no," he said. "But together, with an army at our backs, she will fall." Nodding in agreement, they set off once more down the path, with the dead in tow, their keen wails echoing across the vast plains. In her mind, Papa Keita raged, his desire for revenge growing with each step.

They came upon the construct suddenly. One moment the cobblestone path stretched on beyond her sight, vanishing in the gloom, the next, it branched off. One way continued into the darkness, the other gave way to a gravel path that gently rose toward a sickly green hedge, a terracotta roof of a large domus peeking out just above it. "Is she there?" asked Lucilla, "and what do we do if she is not?"

"We will do what she did to us," he said. "Tear down her stronghold; destroy everything she holds dear; force her to face us."

"To destruction," whispered Lucilla, raising a hand above her head, the deads' haunting wails fading to silence, the deathly quiet sending shivers up and down her spine. Her mind was not fully merged with the vodun, and some small part of her was full of doubt, questioning that madness of attacking a creature hundreds of years old who had dealings with creatures that existed before the dawn of humanity, but she relished in the notion that it was her choice, that live or die, it would be her who decided her fate. Without fanfare, she let her hand fall, and the dead surged forward, their keening howls leaving her dazed for a heartbeat.

"By the gods!" she said, her jaw falling open as the faceless shades pouring ahead of her exploded in a flash of gray-blue ash against an unseen barrier, their forms crackling like lightning and then vanishing. She slowed her pace, worrying with each step. The damned were meant to draw out defenses they were not aware of, overwhelming with sheer numbers, but the barrier held, not weakening with their onslaught. She was about to pull back, calling off the attack when she had a flash of insight—the dead did not belong here. They were from the outside, but Lucilla was a different matter. Raising her chin, she steepled her palms above her head and shouted a Sandawei word of power from deep in her new memories. With a rush of wind, the dead attacking the barrier parted, moving without moving. Squaring her shoulders, she strode to the barrier, regal despite wearing little more than a grime-covered stola.

"What are you doing?" said Papa Keita when she stopped in front of the barrier, reaching out with a trembling hand. "You do not know. You do not know."

Lucilla could feel the vodun fighting her, attempting to force her hand to stillness, but the body was still hers, bound to her will despite his powerful presence. "They think me weak. They all did, expecting me to die among the damned. Now I will show them how wrong they were." She shouted with glee when her arm passed through the barrier, the itan on her arms glowing bright. Plunging both arms through, a jolt ran through her when she spread her arms wide, pushing the barrier open enough for a river of the damned to flow through.

"She is ours now," shouted Papa Keita, in her mind, and Lucilla smiled, her flowing crown of brown hair caught by the wind, whipping behind her as she strode through the barrier after her army, then letting the makeshift door collapse behind her to face her death or destiny, which, she couldn't be sure.

SEVENTEEN

THE BAOBAB

The bodies hung like rotting fruit from the once proud baobab, impaled across the skeletal branches that spread shade and comfort to the village beneath it. "How can the Nok live like this?" she asked, hugging herself.

Guardian Shoyebi sighed, his body stiff. "They are only visible to those who can see the weave, the chosen, and some others. Everyone else sees only the bare branches."

"Who, what are they?" asked Vesper, unable to tear her eyes away from the nightmare.

"They are the shades of our fallen enemies, transformed into pure Ase," said Shoyebi. "Some of our dead as well. Those who chose to be sacrificed for the greater good."

"You do this to your own people?" she asked, bile rising in the back of her throat. "That's monstrous!"

"What would you know of monstrous!" he said, his jaw clenching. "You grew up under the wonders of a healthy baobab, your belly full, never wanting for anything."

Vesper tore her eyes away from the horrible tree, frowning at the guardian. "What could have made you do such a thing, to make you think this was anything but cruel beyond cruel. Even the Sandawei would not do something so evil."

"Do not compare us to the Sandawei; we are nothing like them," he said, his body shaking. "And you Ose are not much better. Your ancient conflicts with them are part of what drove us to this."

Vesper's eyes narrowed, and she took a step away from him while focusing the Ase in her blood, channeling it through her skin and muscle, her eyes hunting for a way to escape. "You think we Ose are responsible for this! Have you lost your mind?"

"Have you?" said Shoyebi, his eyes widening at the subtle glow from the patterns on her arms. "If you knew anything of your history, you would know better."

"Enlighten me," she said in a flat tone, looking around her, her brow narrowing when she saw that the villagers were going about their day as if nothing were amiss.

"Why do you think your people were thrown out of the garden? The constant warring between you and the Sandawei drew all the first peoples into your conflict, forcing us to take sides in a battle we had no desire to fight."

"I don't believe you."

The guardian blew out his cheeks, pressing his lips together. "Is it not true that even now, centuries later, your conflict rages on? Do you even know why you hate them?"

Vesper bared her teeth, balling her fists. "They killed Magda. Their agents forced the Romans to kill every last Ose... my people are no more because of them."

They arrived at the foot of the great tree, and Vesper forgot the argument for a moment, gasping at the fragile bark and flaking wood, fearing that if she touched it, the whole tree would crumble to dust. "No, that is now, in the present day," said Shoyebi, caressing its bark ever so softly, like a parent brushing the cheek of a child. "But it was so long ago, few remember. All I know is that you and they are violent, not caring who you hurt in your desire for vengeance."

"We Ose are peaceful," she scoffed. "Not driven by conquest like the Sandawei. They are the ones bringing blight to the world."

"Yet you prepare for battle, for violence instead of trying to understand, negotiate with wisdom and peace," he said with a frown.

Vesper pursed her lips, wanting him to be wrong but knowing he was right. Her shoulders slumped as she let the Ase coursing through her skin and muscle dissipate back into her blood. "Apologies, Guardian," she said, looking away in shame. "Magda raised me to be better than that. I think I have spent too much time among the Romans."

"It is understandable; their bloodlust is infectious," said Shoyebi. "Come, I will show you what we have done... and why." She nodded, and he led her to the massive crack at the heart of the tree, motioning that she should follow.

Vesper was not sure what to expect when she entered the dimly lit space, but after her eyes adjusted, her brow shot up in wonder, never having imagined such a thing. The interior of the baobab was massive, and while the exterior of the great tree was covered in blight and rot, the inside was full of life, lit by a soft emerald glow from high above. "It's beautiful," she said, her gaze following a wide set of stairs that circled along the trunk, rising higher than she could see, connecting to platforms that appeared not to have been built apart, but grown from the tree itself. The Nok congregated in these spaces, talking, drinking and laughing, all as if it were some grand city square.

Shoyebi beamed with pride, puffing out his chest. "Despite what you may think, this is a place of harmony, of peace and community. My people have found a balance with nature."

She forced her face to stillness, not wanting to judge before she gave him a chance to show her the truth. "You promised you would make me understand," said Vesper, her nerves settling as she drew in lungfuls of sweet, almost seductive air that she recognized as the blossom of the flower of the baobab.

The guardian nodded, leading her away from the joyous

cacophony, down a sloping path that took them deep into the bowels of the tree, where it was darker, cooler. They arrived at a large opening to find Seye waiting for them, his square features looking sinister in the dim light that came from a series of vines that crawled along the walls. "The others are waiting," he said, ignoring Vesper, his attention focused on his mentor. "They are ready."

"Good good," he said, bobbing his head. "This should explain much."

Vesper entered the chamber to find a small cluster of women and men of all ages, each one of them dressed in the red robes she had seen out in the fields, channeling Ase. The guardian nodded, and they raised their Ase-covered arms, and the geometric patterns began to glow, coming to life, bending and spinning, intertwining until she couldn't distinguish where one began and the other finished. The dim room was suddenly bright, forcing her to squint as her eyes adjusted. Then, just as quickly, it was dark once more, the only light coming from a canopy of twinkling stars that somehow brought the tapestry of night underneath the great tree. "What's all of this," she asked.

"Look... truly look," whispered Shoyebi.

Vesper stared deeply at the reflection of the night sky, her brows coming together when she found none of the familiar patterns or constellations she knew. When she focused, looking for the subtle images that should have been the weave, she was taken aback. "This is not the history I have seen in the night sky," she said, looking for herself, her aunt, and her family. Not finding them in this unfamiliar tapestry. "This is different. The connections do not go beyond this place."

Shoyebi nodded. "What else do you see? Follow the threads."

Vesper's eyes flicked back to the guardian and then back at the tapestry, her stomach turning with worry at what she might find. She did as she was told, following the threads that connected mothers to daughters, fathers to sons. Going from family to family, following the bloodlines back through the distant past, at last understanding when she came to the beginning. "This is impossible, this tapestry. The lives it connects do not go very far back."

"Even after the Ose and the Sandawei were cast out of the garden, the doorway to hate among the first people stayed firmly open. It was an infection that we could not cure, and with that door open... something came through."

"By Olodumare," said Vesper, cringing at the pain in his voice, looking at the guardian, to find tears rolling down his face.

"As our hate grew, the corruption grew with it, tainting the weave. Whatever came through brought madness and more hate. It was not long before the tapestry was tattered and torn. It was slow at first, but then spread faster with each passing year."

"What did you do?" she whispered, already knowing the answer.

Guardian Shoyebi sighed, squaring his shoulders. "Most of the great baobabs were all but gone near the end. The Nok, we were lucky, our tree was still vibrant, strong like her people. It held back the taint somewhat, but with madness growing, we had to do something."

Vesper returned her attention to the projection of stars above her, focusing on the beginning of the tapestry, her mind delving deeper and deeper, seeing the events unfold as if she were there. "I can see it... after a great battle," she said, swallowing hard. "Bodies, broken and beaten, as far as the eye can see."

"Yes, dead, but connected, their potential still there."

"Potential springs from all things," said Vesper, repeating one of the first lessons her Aunt Magda had taught her. "In the rock, the tree, even the dirt under our feet has potential, power."

A flash of anger crossed Shoyebi's face, and he raised a fist. "We took those bodies, every last one. We dug deep into the roots of our baobab, casting them down deep in the earth. We took our own, too, those that had fallen. Any who were willing."

Vesper saw it, ancient chosen using their last connections to a tattered weave, boring beneath this very tree, nestling the dead among its roots, weaving their connections together. The great baobab exploding with Ase as potential and power burned from its roots, spreading through its leaves, flooding it with energy. "You bound them to the tree."

"And more."

Vesper cursed under her breath when she delved deeper, feeling like she was almost there. She felt the earth under her feet as she and all of the Nok gathered under the shade of the great tree. Thousands upon thousands of people shuddering with pain and pleasure as the chosen wandered among them, marking their bodies with Ashe symbols, their arms and legs covered in the geometric patterns. "Do they know? Do your people know?" she asked, shaking her head.

"No," said the guardian, his voice devoid of emotion. "Few living do."

It felt as if she were there, under the shade of the great tree. She watched in rapture as a chosen bonded with the baobab, a thick emerald cord of Ase forming between them that glowed like the sun at midday. The cord stretched out as he then wandered around those kneeling before him, his touch connecting them, to him, to the baobab, to each other, and nothing else.

"Do you understand now?" asked Shoyebi.

Vesper put a hand to her chest, the missing connection to Narcissus more profound with the revelation. "You created your own weave, cutting yourself off from the rest of humanity."

"Yes... and it worked for a time," he said. "The remaining first peoples died off; we thought it a victory. The darkness that had plagued us vanished, disappearing along with what was left of the weave. The garden followed not long after, leaving the desert you see today."

"And now..." she said, eyeing the fraying threads of the current day, seeing the turbulent times coming.

Shoyebi bowed his head, looking old and beaten down. "Now our baobab is dying, and every single man, woman, and child you saw will die with it!"

"Then you lied to bring me here?" snapped Vesper, her eyes narrowing. "Why?"

"Not entirely, I promise. You will receive training. It is my responsibility to be your guardian."

"But there's more?"

The guardian bit his lower lip, his voice falling to little more than a whisper: "Yes, our connection with the weave is gone, while you still follow the old ways. We brought you here in hopes... in the hope that together we can reconnect to the world, before it's too late."

EIGHTEEN
THE CELT

"Now you look like a proper Roman, a man of distinction worthy of being doctore to Caesar himself."

Narcissus stood on the sands of the open-roofed training ground somewhere in the imperial palace, shaking with rage, his beard gone. He had never felt such shame in his life, had never felt like less of a man. "Your death will be well earned, Commodus. I swear it." Commodus had called a visit to his private barber a gift, that cleaning up his appearance would be a way to elevate him above the other slaves. To Narcissus it was just Commodus exerting his cruelty, belittling him by making him look like less of a man.

"Tsk tsk," said Commodus, rattling a chain wrapped around his hand. "You will call me Caesar, or your bent-backed friend here will die in the most painful way."

He looked at Linus, who sat hunched over a low stool, a chain circling his neck as if he were a hound. Looking away from his friend, he squared his massive shoulders, locking eyes with Commodus so there would be no doubt to his threat. "Your death will be well earned... Caesar."

Commodus pulled hard on the chain, wrenching Linus off the

ground so that they could see eye to eye. "You see that, Linus? Even the most stubborn Celt can be made to listen. It is a shame his words will kill you one day."

Despite having the life choked from him, Linus was silent except for the smallest of choking noises, never blinking as he met the emperor's eyes. Narcissus knew that with his bent back, the old gladiator was in pain beyond imagining, but he never gave in, never gave the emperor the satisfaction of the slightest whimper. Commodus held him a moment longer before letting him fall, frowning at the old gladiator before returning his attention to Narcissus. "You should be grateful for my kindness, that in my mercy I let you speak to me in such a way. Any other slave would be punished in the most painful manner," he said, his eyes flicking back and forth between the two men. "But it doesn't matter, I shall punish your woman instead. It won't be long until she grows to enjoy my touch."

Spittle rolled down Narcissus's bare chin, his face red and splotchy, as he took a single step forward. "If you touch her—"

"You will do nothing!" he snapped, rattling the chain once more. "If you harm one hair on our godly person, Cleander here has orders for her to be fed to the lions, but not after she does a tour in Rome's worst brothels."

Narcissus halted; his eyes locked on the swarthy Praetorian prefect who had become the emperor's right hand. At the mention of Vesper, he smiled, resting a hand on the gaudy weapon on his hip, a gladius he had won by killing the former prefect. "It would be my honor... Caesar."

"I want to see her again—up close this time. To speak with her," he said, letting out a slow breath.

Commodus shook his head, offering the Celt a knowing smile. "Given how much trouble the pair of you have made, I would be a fool to do such a thing. No, not until you are properly broken: only then will I give you that chance."

The big man choked back his words, knowing that Commodus would be true to his threats, and whatever he said would only cause

Vesper pain. Resting a hand on his stomach, he once again cursed their absent bond. He could no longer feel her, having no choice but to take the words of these fools, that she was alive and well. When they were first connected, he could feel every emotion, every brush against her skin, and feared he would go mad. Now that it was gone, he feared the same madness from her absence. "Apologies... Caesar," he said at last, his muscles feeling like water as his anger cooled.

"Very good," he said, mounting the steps to an elevated podium, where he watched the day's training on the sands. The open courtyard was at least the same size as the training grounds of the Ludus Magnus, with sloped seating for guests built into one side, just below where the emperor sat. Instead of training, Commodus spent his day joking with his guards while watching with a keen eye as the big Celt went through the motions battling with slaves or the occasional Praetorian guard, all so that Commodus could learn how Narcissus fought so well with just his bare hands. When he had his fill of watching, Commodus himself would join in the training, never against Narcissus, fighting with some poor soul, applying what he'd learned from watching the big Celt, then when he grew bored, retiring to the baths for other amusements. He spent little time ruling, leaving Cleander and a few other sycophants to run the day-to-day.

"What's all of this?" grumbled Narcissus, rubbing his beardless chin when their routine changed, as a dozen men dressed in silk tunics and brightly colored togas shuffled in, taking seats on the stone benches just below the emperor, all of them casting worried glances at him while arguing in hushed tones.

They fell silent when Commodus stood to his full height, glaring down on them. "Senators, that you believe you have enough merit to sit so high... is an insult to the lowborn of Rome," he said, waving over a pair of Praetorian guards, who stood watch at the entrance of the training ground. The senators offered weak protests as the black-and-purple-clad men hurried them from their seats, forcing them to the lowest level, directly on the sands.

Narcissus laughed in amusement, frowning at their gray hair and wrinkled skin, disgusted at their skinny chests and fat faces. He moved to stand in front of them, his towering presence frightening them to silence. "How can so much power rest in the hands of such weak men?"

They all stared in silence until one of them found his courage, a bronzed-skin man in a reddish-brown toga draped over his arm stood, looking up to Commodus. "Caesar," he began with a snort, "I am a senator of Rome, not some common plebeian. How dare this barbarian have the gall to address me so? I demand that he be flogged."

The emperor sat down, taking the time to settle in his seat while the senator's nostrils flared. "Senator Sabinus," he began, a feral smile growing on his face while the senator held his toga in a white-knuckled grip, "Narcissus may be a slave... but he is my slave. In my eyes, this places him well above you. In fact, we agree with his words. You are, in fact, a weak, useless man."

"Insolent boy! I have served the empire since before you were born," began the senator, only to fall silent, swallowing hard when Commodus stood, taking a step down from his perch.

"Senator, you are here to witness my greatness, so you will behave with respect. I do not wish to make examples of you," he said, starting to remove his tunic just as a Praetorian guard appeared with the golden lion's mane, the costume he often wore when he appeared in the arena while another man brought him the massive club he often fought with. Throwing the club over his shoulder, he strode down the stairs, the senators' faces flushing when they saw that the emperor wore only a golden loincloth to match the lion's mane he had been favoring these last few months.

Narcissus stepped back to give Commodus space while he took a few practice swings, the senators flinching back each time the massive club whistled in their direction. Watching the weapon with eyes as wide as saucers, Senator Sabinus rose on unsteady legs. "Caesar," he began, coughing into his hand, "you cannot just kill us; to do so would not be in the best interest of the empire. The Senate administers—"

Commodus sprung forward, slamming the club into a training post near their seats, splintering the tall wooden rod driven into the sand. "You were saying something," he said, returning his attention to the dark-bronzed-skin senator who fell into his seat as if he had fainted, the other men forced to hold him up.

"What do you intend?" asked Narcissus in a low voice, approaching Commodus as if he were a rabid dog.

"You see these men," said Commodus, his broad chest heaving as he pointed to the senators. "They are not warriors, like us. They're parasites who've spent decades getting fat and rich, profiting from my father's wars while they have never swung a sword or dug a ditch, and now that I have stopped their wars and brought peace to the empire for the first time in a century, they want my head, but I'll show them; they will learn what it means to challenge me."

Narcissus nodded along, keeping his face still. "What will you do with them?" he asked, not wanting to be included in whatever madness he was planning. It was often like this with Commodus: one minute he would threaten murder, the next he would speak like they were staunch allies.

"I intend to put what I have learned from you to good use. Now sit, and watch."

"As you wish," said Narcissus, doing as he was told, taking a seat off to the side by himself, far away from the frightened senators.

Commodus threw away his club, flexing his well-muscled arms in anticipation of fighting with just his hands and feet. "Bring out the first set," he shouted, nodding to one of his guardsmen. The big Celt cursed under his breath when a heavy wooden door swung open at the rear of the training grounds, and a group of men in heavy iron chains shuffled forward, many of them raising hands to shield their eyes from the sun, squinting like they had been too long in the dark. The group stopped in the center of the training area, and Commodus walked up and down the line, squeezing an arm, poking them in their chests, or forcing open their mouths while he inspected their teeth. "Unchain them; these will do."

A tired-looking legionnaire in worn armor and a tattered, red cloak emerged from the wooden door, unlocking the chains, then vanishing once more through the door until at least returning with an array of rusted weapons that he threw on the sands. "Survive and see another day," he said in a harsh tone, shrugging at the unchained men. The slaves darted forward, arming themselves with what they could. Warped spears and bent blades, many of them notched and splintered from previous battles, dried blood still visible on the dull blades.

"Kill me and go free!" shouted Commodus, spreading his arms wide while turning in a circle while the men cast nervous glances at one another.

A pale, thick-chested Gaul, with a filthy beard and gray-streaked hair exploded into action, holding a rough-hewn spear with enough expertise to mark him as a soldier of some sort. He attacked Commodus with deadly purpose, threatening with a series of quick thrusts that the emperor just managed to dodge, flashing a brilliant smile to the senators when the Gaul warrior spun on his back heel, clipping Commodus on the chin with the blunt end of the weapon, to little effect. He came at him again, feinting to the right and then aiming for the emperor's belly. Commodus caught the spear in one hand, the Gaul's eyes popping open in surprise when his weapon was snapped in half. Commodus followed up with a wicked jab, snapping the surprised man's head back with enough force to send him tumbling onto his back. Unconscious or dead, Narcissus couldn't be sure.

Seeing that the emperor was serious, the other men charged in, some of them working in pairs, others alone. It was clear that the men were chosen because they had some sort of skill in war. Two of the men attacked in unison, hoping to gain some advantages with their numbers, one man using his gladius in a series of short thrusts, while his partner swung wide, both of them catching only air as Commodus followed Narcissus's lessons to perfection, anticipating the attacks before they came, then countering with vicious punches and kicks when his attackers were caught flat-footed and blindsided when he was no longer where they expected him to be.

Narcissus found himself impressed when the emperor spun in place to catch a charging Syrian spearman by the throat, effortlessly knocking aside the razor-sharp tip that was aimed for his heart. He lifted the man from his feet, all the while looking at the sitting senators, then finally hurling him like he was a child, "Is this the best you can do!" he shouted, waving the slaves on while letting his arms fall to his sides.

The slaves attacked with their crude weapons while Commodus did nothing, throwing back his head in mocking laughter when their swords and spears broke against his skin, leaving not a blemish or trace of blood. "You see!" he shouted, turning to face the senators with his arms held wide while the slaves beat on his back. "I am a god. The weapons of man cannot harm me. I will—" A gladius-wielding slave slapped the flat end of his blade to the emperor's face, not hurting him, but shocking him to silence. "Insolent wretch!" said Commodus, unleashing a wicked backhand to the man's face, the blow knocking him off his feet. "You think you can hurt me! You will all pay for your arrogance!"

Narcissus had seen violence in his lifetime, more than he ever wanted to. Thus, he was hardened to the hurt men inflicted on one another, but what the emperor did to those men when he unleashed his fury on them, was beyond anything he had ever witnessed, even on the sands of the Colosseum. He looked away, swallowing hard when the echo of breaking bones reached his ear. His face flushing with shame while the slaves screamed for mercy, begging and pleading for death. The training grounds fell silent for a heartbeat, and Narcissus thought that it was over, but when he opened his eyes, he found the emperor striding toward the senators, his hands covered in gore.

"Look at me!" he shouted, pulling Senator Sabinus to his feet, staining his toga with blood. "You had the nerve to challenge me in the Senate, and now you don't have the courage to see my glory, to learn my greatness!"

The senator cringed, spittle coming from his mouth as he fell to his knees while raising his hands defensively over his head. "P-please, merciful Caesar, I beg your forgiveness."

"If you wish my forgiveness, you must do one thing for me."

"Anything," said Sabinus, his body shaking.

"You will convene the Senate, as you are now, no delays. You will tell the other senators what you witnessed here today, confess your fears, your doubts. If you do this, I will allow you to keep your estate, your position. I will even leave you permission to play at being rulers of Rome."

The shaking senator glanced back toward his peers, all of whom hurriedly nodded, their wide eyes never blinking. "This very day, Caesar."

"Good, good," he said, letting the senator go, forgotten, while he wiped blood and gore from his chest and well-defined stomach. "Well, this deserves some time in the baths, don't you think, Narcissus?"

The big Celt froze, his stomach clenching when Commodus raised an expectant eyebrow while looking him up and down. The senators halted their leaving, each one of them stopping to watch. The rattle of chains from the podium broke the silence as Linus stood up from his bench. "Apologies, Caesar," he said, clearing his throat. "Narcissus is too proud to speak of such things, but his tastes do not lie in that way. He has eyes only for Vesper."

"One woman? Are you a madman?"

"It is the way of both of our peoples," said Narcissus.

Commodus tapped his chin, his eyes narrowing when he locked eyes with him. "I could force you...," he said, letting the threat hang in the air.

Narcissus sucked in a deep breath, shifting his stance in preparation. "Not while I live."

They locked eyes, and Narcissus was sure he would carry out his threat, but then the emperor's eyes took on a milky sheen, and a heartbeat later, his smile returned as though the threat had never happened. "You are a brave man. I will not spoil you with my base instincts. Retire to your rooms. I will find my amusement elsewhere."

The training ground was silent except for the rattle of chains as a Praetorian guardsman brought Linus to him, Commodus vanishing down a wide hall moments later. When he was gone, Narcissus fell back onto his seat, burying his head in his hands, amazed that he still lived, swearing to himself over and over again that the emperor would die at his hand, no matter the cost.

NINETEEN
THE DYING

Shoyebi was true to his word, and Vesper began training the very next day with the rising sun. She had expected to be learning about the weave, about Ase, and the true nature of the world. Perhaps even going on some wild adventure, jumping to exotic places like his apprentice Seye. Instead, the guardian took her to a green field cordoned off from the village about the size of the Colosseum. Here, she found one section covered with straw men lined up to be used as targets, and large rocks, many larger than a pack mule, piled into a neat pyramid. The rest strangely reminded her of home, with wild-flowers, pungent spices of all kinds scattered among low bushes and small trees filled with exotic fruit, hanging heavy from the branches.

"You do not look impressed," said a lanky man striding toward them wearing a long, colorful tunic that hung past his calves.

Vesper nodded while looking around the near empty field. "Apologies, I expected something more... exotic."

"Look deeper, your eyes can deceive, but the heart never does!" he said with a beaming smile, offering her his hand. "I am Oroku! It is my duty to lead you to the wisdom and peace of the great god."

"O-of course," said Vesper, taking his hand, a smile coming to her face as he shook it excitedly. She couldn't help but stare; he was different from the other Nok she had seen in the village. He was light skinned with a narrow face and hawkish eyes that never seemed to blink, while his tight-knit hair was matted and long, falling ropelike past the center of his back, his nose pointed and narrow.

"Good, good. It has been too long since we have had some new blood. Some fresh ideas," he said, frowning at Shoyebi.

"Gratitude, I—" began Vesper, only to fall silent when Oroku pursed his lips, his eyes opening wide, like saucers.

"The Ashe of the Ose," he whispered, his words full of awe "Together with the mark of Eshu. I never thought to see such a thing in my life," he said, his eyes drifting toward the stars tattooed across her collarbone and throat.

"Ashe?"

"Yes, they are symbols of power, of lineage," he said, lifting the sleeves of his tunic to reveal an interlocking, teardrop pattern covering his arms, flowing to his upper chest. "They are different for each of the first people."

"You are not of the Nok," she said, having a flash of insight when she looked back and forth between him and Shoyebi.

"Oroku and his people are allies, friends."

"Do not start with your lies, Shoyebi," said Oroku, rolling his eyes. "The girl would learn the truth soon enough anyway. My people, the Berbers, are subject to the Nok. Not that we can be called a people anymore; we are a remnant of a remnant. A dying ember that will soon fade from the world."

"Enough!" said Shoyebi, his nostrils flaring. "Vesper is here to join with the others, to learn our ways in hopes that she can help us, not listen to your grievances."

Orouk frowned like he'd swallowed something bitter. "You mean help you," he accused.

Feeling like the two men were about to come to blows, Vesper stepped between them. "Master Oroku, I have so many questions. I'm not sure where to start," said Vesper, smiling at him once more.

"It is just Oroku, and while I applaud your desire for wisdom and peace, we must wait for the others," he said finally, returning her smile, his voice calm despite the hard look that passed between him and Shoyebi.

Vesper started to look for others making their way to the cordoned-off area, when her hackles rose. A cool mist appeared from nowhere, rolling across the green field, vague humanoid shapes appearing in the fog, surrounding her. Instinctively, she summoned a gladius and shield, holding the blade in a reverse grip to better use it in close combat. She opened her mouth to ask Shoyebi what was going on, when the shapes materialized fully, and Vesper cursed under her breath, banishing her armaments when she realized they were like her: young people here for training, each of them with a guardian at their side, hovering around them protectively.

"Who are they?" she asked Oroku in a low voice.

"They are like you," he said, nodding to each of the guardians in turn as they appeared. "Apprentices... the chosen of the Nok."

"What about the chosen of the Berbers... your children?"

Oroku's smile faded, his voice cracking when he spoke. "As I said, my people are a dying ember. Now, line up with the others; we shall begin today's lessons."

She couldn't help but feel alone as they lined up, with the guardians standing at the ready behind their apprentices. Not knowing what to do, she stood dumbfounded before Shoyebi pushed her along so she could fall in line. "Am I your apprentice?" she asked over her shoulder to the guardian, who stood behind her with a stone look on his face.

"Of course you are," he said matter-of-factly, dismissing her question with a snort. "Our training will give you much needed discipline, control. You will no longer be wild and wasteful."

Despite the early morning heat, a chill ran through her as she eyed the others. Just by the way they held themselves, the way they dressed, she couldn't help but worry that she would not hold up against them. Vesper had put aside the leather vest and long tunic she normally wore for a simple linen dress and homespun headscarf to cover her braids, but she felt provincial when comparing herself to the other chosen's' fine clothing. The boys wore wide-sleeved agbada robes that fell past their ankles, gray and somber but with complex patterns running down their chests, while the girls wore robes of similar length but were more colorful: sky blue, deep oranges, and striking red silks covered in gold-and-silver geometric patterns along the sleeves and bosom.

There were six of them, three boys and three girls, and they all seemed so serious, with their chins held high and arms locked behind their backs or tucked away in their sleeves, like they were Roman nobles looking down on her. She had been excited about delving into her power, but looking at the other chosen, she was consumed with doubt, wanting nothing more than to train alone. Without thinking, she fully opened herself to the world around her, when she under-stood Oroku's words, that she should look deeper. The garden was very much like her Aunt Magda's. Powerful filaments of Ase flowed all around her, snaking from the bushes at the end of the training grounds to the fruit trees and beyond. She shuddered with pleasure as she drew deep, reaching to touch a thread that would lead back to the baobab tree at the heart of the village, preparing to jump, only to gasp in shock when the glowing line of power at her fingertips vanished, and she could see only darkness.

"Enough of that," said Shoyebi in a harsh whisper. "This is not our way; the only Ase we draw comes from our baobab."

"Wh-what's happening?" she said with her breath coming in short spurts.

"You cannot touch what you cannot see."

"Yes, but—"

"You belong here just as much as they do," he said, reading her thoughts. "They may look the part, but you possess a deeper power. Trust me, you will see soon enough that you can draw on sources of Ase they can only dream of."

A wave of relief washed over her as her sight returned, and she could feel the warmth of the sun on her skin once more. "Apologies. I have been on my own for so long, I have forgotten what it was like to have a teacher," she said, focusing her attention on the Oroku, who paced back and forth, eyeing them all with an intense stare.

She wondered when the training would begin when commotion behind them drew her attention. She looked over her shoulder to see Seye arriving, the square-jawed seeker's eyes never leaving her, a half-smile coming to his face when he took a spot next to her.

"Now that we are all here, we can begin," said Oroku, locking his arms behind his back. "The almighty Olodumare has given you a great honor! You have been given the gift of Aṣẹ, the power to unleash the potential in the world as no others can. Now, if you are lucky and learn well, some of you will have the honor of defending our people.

Vesper's brow drew together as she whispered over her shoulder to Shoyebi, "What do you need defending from? I thought that all of the other first peoples died out or left."

Shoyebi cleared his throat, hesitating before he answered, "There are threats beyond people, dangers that spawn from the void that surrounds us."

"Are you with us?" asked Oroku, suddenly in front of Vesper, with a warm smile.

"Apologies," she said. "I am."

"I will leave you in Oroku's care," said Shoyebi, nodding to the other guardians, who parted as a group, vanishing on threads of Ase that connected to other parts of the village.

The lanky man nodded to her, continuing in a lecturing tone, "I was saying that while I will show you the basics, you will spend the day observing, as the others in this group have mastered this art and spend their days in advanced lessons, learning how to attack and defend with their Ashe."

"Of course," said Vesper. "I will try to learn quickly."

Oroku ordered the others to pair off against one another, while he and Seye took her some distance away before he began. "It would be best if you observed this from the world of the *emi*, with the sight."

Vesper shook her head, not understanding. "Emi?"

Seye raised his chin, looking down his nose at her. "It is what you Romans call the spirit. It is where one can see the connections that make up the world."

"I understand," said Vesper, crossing her arms under her breasts. "But something must be wrong with your sight. I am clearly not Roman."

"You Ose have spent generations suckling at the teats of Rome's emperors, wasting precious Ase in service to their wars, loyal servants used to expand their corrupt empire."

Vesper's first impulse was to lash out, to attack with insults of her own, but then she recalled Shoyebi's words. That Seye was a blunt instrument and that she had shamed him by being victorious in their brief battle. Instead, she smiled at him as one would a small child throwing a tantrum, turning her attention to Oroku. "Please begin your lesson. I am eager to learn."

Oroku smiled, his eyes twinkling with amusement. "Very well, let us begin. Watch."

"Gratitude," she said, shifting her vision as instructed, taking note of every thread, every connection.

The emerald line that connected the lanky Berber to the baobab grew thicker than her arm as he directed the potential to a tear-shaped symbol on his arm, the pattern coming alive, growing as if it were a seed springing from the earth, reaching for the sun. Oroku cleared his throat as the pattern began to take shape, that of a simple glowing sphere that she had seen once before. "Anything can be constructed this way; simple items are the easiest; you only have to have the will to hold the image in your mind."

Vesper smiled when he tied off the thread, locking the Ase used in the pattern when the image of the sphere returned to his flesh, now a tool to be called on when needed. "Whatever I can imagine?" she asked, her mind filling with ideas.

Oroku nodded. "It is easier with simple objects," he said, showing her the many images on his flesh. "But it is said that those with the proper will can create anything. Now, watch, I will do it once more."

"No, I understand how it is done," she said, opening herself to the flow of Ase in her blood, drawing on small amounts from the garden surrounding her. Closing her eyes, she directed the power through one of the many concentric patterns dotting her arms.

"Arrogant Ose," muttered Seye, shaking his head. "Thinking to master our ways after a single lesson."

Ignoring him, she formed the image of a gladius in her mind, picturing its steel blade, razor sharp, the tip of the fine weapon strong enough to pierce bone, armor, and more. She could almost feel the smooth leather of its hilt, with the bright metal of the cross guard glowing in the morning sun. The image was almost complete when she cocked her head, a thought running through her mind. Letting the Ase dissipate to nothingness, she opened her eyes. "Does it have to be a normal item?" she asked, her gaze darting between the two men in front of her.

"As I told you, it's not so simple!" said Seye with a smirk on his face.

"I have done this often enough, in my own way," said Vesper, hints of annoyance creeping into her tone.

The seeker rolled his eyes, but Oroku's response was different, smiling and nodding with approval. "It can be done, but often by those with many years of experience."

Vesper's belly bubbled with excitement as a memory burned through her mind, a memory of a battle and how she'd won. "I have fought with the Sandawei... more than once," she said, keeping her eyes open this time as she resumed the process of pouring Ase into one of the concentric patterns, the Ashe on her arm, the image of her gladius made of pure light forming in her mind. "At every turn they have drawn power from beyond the weave, a dark place that is cold, empty, an infinite void."

"They were much the same before the Nok exiled them. Olodumare's punishment drove them to dark places," said Oroku in a hushed tone.

"Keep silent, old man," said Seye, sneering at him.

"Many times when I battled them, I could see their connections to this dark power. It is not so different from the threads that make up our weave," continued Vesper. "The times when I managed to defeat them, I summoned a gladius made of light, using it to cut their connection to the void."

Seye began to pace back and forth in front of them, his nostrils flaring. "Do you think us fools!" he rasped, the veins in his neck throbbing. "The ancient texts tell of such things. We have followed them, only to learn that one must have a connection to the void to do it, and only the Sandawei know such things."

A flash of light burst into being as Vesper finished forming the gladius, while all around the training ground, the other students stopped, their eyes locked on to what she had summoned. The gladius was unlike anything she had created before. Its blade was a brilliant, polished steel with concentric patterns that matched those on her arms, spread up and down its length, with motes of light glowing a cool amber even in the morning sun. "I did it," she said, her voice shaking while beads of sweat rolled off her temples.

"Tie it off!" said Oroku. "Quickly!"

She did as she was told, spinning together the threads of Ase she had used to construct the weapon, locking them into an infinite loop that held the potential in the pattern she had imagined. "By Olodu-mare, I wish Narcissus could see this!" she said, returning the weapon to the simple pattern on her arm and then summoning it again immediately.

"May I," said Oroku, taking the weapon from her hands, his voice full of reverence.

"Do you really think such simple tricks will save us?" growled Seye, glaring at her while continuing to pace. "Didn't you hear her? The Ose whore will take what we teach her to her Roman masters. She has no intention of helping us."

Vesper pressed her lips together, breathing in through her nose to control her irritation. "I have done nothing to wrong you, seeker, and have no desire to do you harm," she said, using his title in hopes that it would calm him. "But I will not let you continue to disrespect me."

"You are not worthy to learn our ways!" he spat. "I will not let it happen, not when I can end you!"

"Wisdom from peace, peace from wisdom," said Oroku in a hurried voice, stepping between them. "This is not our way."

Seye grabbed the lanky man by his tunic, throwing him to the ground. "Peace is your way, foolish Berber, not mine!" he said, drawing the heavy-bladed, hooked sword he carried on his back.

On the ground Oroku scrambled away, looking to other chosen, who stood with their mouths agape, their eyes unblinking. "Don't just stand there!" he yelled. "Go to your guardians. Find Shoyebi!"

The others vanished like morning mist as Vesper recalled the gladius she had just created, channeling the Ase coursing through her veins into her skin and strength. "Are you sure you want to do this? The last time you ended up on your knees with my blade at your throat."

"I was told you were an untrained child," he said, spinning his blade. "But this time I'm ready for you! I won't make the same mistake again."

Vesper smiled, grateful for her time in the ludus, knowing that to underestimate anyone was a sure way to meet your end. "Then I promise you a merciful death."

The young seeker's face twisted with rage as he lunged for her, his heavy blade hissing as he swung it in wide arcs, back and forth, aiming for her belly, while Vesper retreated slowly, step by step, pulling her gladius in tight to deflect his relentless attacks, their weapons sparking blue and white with every clash.

"Stop this!" shouted Oroku, his voice nothing more than a distant echo as Vesper fell into an easy rhythm, watching and waiting while Seye pounded away with his blade.

Vesper caught Seye's sword with the hilt of her gladius, locking their arms together while trying to push him away, only to double over when his knee found her gut. He raised his blade to separate her neck from her body when she managed to slam an elbow to his chin, sending him staggering back. "Enough games," he said, wiping his mouth while the geometric patterns on his arms came alive, forming a swarm of glowing spheres of all shapes and sizes.

"You tried that before. It didn't work so well," she said, reversing the grip on her gladius to deflect the spheres as she did last time, in the same breath, pulling together threads of Ase from the garden to form a shield, raising it high to defend herself.

Seye looked down his nose at her, shaking his head. "You fight like a Roman," he sneered as his arm shot out, a hail of spheres streaking toward her.

A storm of sparks exploded all around Vesper, driving her back as her shield absorbed the brunt of his assault while she ducked behind it, gritting her teeth through the heat and shock as burning remnants fell on her dark skin. Another wave came at her, and Vesper pivoted, intending to use her sword to deflect the attack, only for Seye to vanish from her sight.

"This is how you intend to fight... like a coward," she said, spinning in place with her shield and gladius pulled in close, keeping one eye on the floating spheres that spun on some invisible axis not far away.

Her mocking words drew him in, and Seye appeared behind her, his heavy blade aimed for her head while a flurry of spheres came at her from the front. Vesper went to one knee, Seye's attack passing harmlessly overhead, while she crouched behind her shield, her arm going numb as she braced against a wave of spheres. Reversing her grip, she stabbed behind her, only to catch air as the seeker vanished once more, and Vesper caught a glimpse of him at the heart of the garden, the Ase on his arms glowing orange and amber, while his face was a mask of concentration. Narrowing her eyes, she shifted her gaze to the world beyond, cursing under her breath when she saw the connection between him and the baobab, which had grown as he drew on more of its strength.

"Run! Run!" screamed Oroku, stumbling to his feet, tearing at her arm to drag her away.

"What is he doing?"

"He intends to burn us all!"

Taking advantage of the distance between them, Vesper reached out, grasping at the thick cord of Ase that stretched between Seye to the great baobab, gooseflesh running up and down her body as she cut him off, shaking with nausea from taking hold of so much rancid potential. "This is over!" she shouted, running toward him after he fell to one knee, slamming his fists to the dirt.

"It is not over," he said, shaking his head as she came closer. "I promise you."

Vesper approached with caution, holding her breath as she stood above him. "Why do you hate me? I have done nothing to you."

"You exist!" he shouted, balling his hands into fists. "You are an affront to every lie the guardians told me! To the sacrifices I have made. To the loved ones I have lost," he finished, his voice full of bile.

She was taken aback, finally understanding. Shoyebi had deceived her from the moment she met him, his lies taking her away from Narcissus and Rome in a desperate attempt to have her help in saving his dying people. But Seye had lived with him for a lifetime. "Blame the guardians, those who deceived you. Not me!"

Seye met her eyes, a chill running down her spine when he smiled at her. "They will pay! Shoyebi more than most," he said, his eyes looking past her.

Following his gaze, Vesper looked around for him to find the guardian stalking toward them, her shoulders slumping in relief when she saw him with Oroku and some of the other young chosen in tow, his face twisted in fury. "Your people will deal with you," she began. "Hopefully they—"

"I watched you, you know," he said, his eyes glittering with hate, "for a long time before, and then after."

"What! Why?"

"To learn, to understand how someone like you could stand against me, defeat me!"

"Then you must know I am not what you think. I am no liar nor a thief!" she said.

The seeker nodded, pushing out his lower lip. "This is true, but it changes nothing... means nothing. Although I am grateful for the time spent, for the wisdom gained."

Vesper opened her mouth to question him further when Shoyebi arrived, pushing her aside. "Arrogant boy! You will be punished for this!" he began, slapping his apprentice hard enough to split his lip.

Seye wiped away the blood from his mouth, glaring at the older man. "You are a liar, Shoyebi! All of you are liars!"

The guardian raised his chin, his nostrils flaring. "No matter how many times I think you have learned your lessons, you disappoint me. Your failures are never ending."

"You will be the first to die, old man," he said, bowing his head while burying his hands in the dirt of the garden. It happened faster than Vesper could react, Shoyebi pulled his arm back to slap him again when he suddenly bent in half, spasming when a stone spear erupted from the earth, driving through his belly and out his back, while a crimson stain soaked through the front of his gold-spun robes.

"How!?" shouted Vesper, jumping back as the garden wilted around her, trees, shrubs, and flowers fading to a dull gray before falling to dust.

"I should thank you," said Seye, climbing to his feet with a snort, laughing as the other chosen fled. "I have learned more in our few encounters than that fool Oroku or any of my teachers have taught me in years."

Vesper backed away, gripping tight to the flow of Ase from the tainted baobab, her breath catching in her throat as the grass beneath her feet blacked to ash. "I didn't think the Nok could draw Ase from anything but their great tree?"

"This is the lie I have lived with," he said, grabbing Shoyebi by the chin so that he could look into his eyes. "The lie he told me over and over again. Shaming me every time I asked why. Now I know, don't I?"

"What do you mean?" she asked, as screams echoed in the distance as the circle of ash spread beyond the field, reaching to the village itself.

"Because they're cowards, aren't you!"

Shoyebi's eyes darted toward Vesper, full of pleading desperation as he fought his apprentice's iron grip as his blood dripped to the ground. "Away from the world. Keep... you... safe... all of you... all of us."

"What are your intentions?" asked Vesper, channeling the massive amount of Ase she was holding, to the sky, thunder booming in the distance as dark clouds rolled in from her efforts.

Seye's gaze hardened as he took a quick glance toward the village, his eyes narrowing as he looked to his guardian. "After I kill this liar," he said, shaking him, "I will kill you. Then burn this place to the ground."

"I cannot allow that," said Vesper, swallowing hard as the storm she summoned flashed overhead, casting them all in an eerie light.

"Then you will die first!

The ground under her feet shook, forcing Vesper to leapt away when jagged shards of stone erupted, tiny slivers cutting into her hardened skin, leaving small gashes along her legs while shredding the long tunic she wore. Skidding to a halt a dozen feet away, she brought her arms down in a chopping motions, showering down crooked fingers of lightning just behind where Seye stood, cursing when the former apprentice vanished, showering Shoyebi with black earth. Knowing how the seeker attacked, Vesper moved quickly, calling down more lighting all around her in hopes of catching him off guard as she ran to see if the guardian was still alive.

"You can't save them," shouted Seye from somewhere behind her as gouts of flame rolled over her, blisters rising on her arms where the flames licked bare skin. Ignoring the pain, Vesper spread her arms wide, blasting away the fire with gusts of wind and rain, the cool water soothing her flesh.

Spotting him running toward the village, Vesper sent waves of Ase through the stars on her collarbone, muttering the ancient words she had learned from Eshu, beads of sweat rolling down her temples as she was no longer alone, an army of her appearing on the rise, taking off in pursuit of the apprentice. "Are you still with us, or has Olodumare taken you," she said, stopping beside the impaled guardian.

"So much... s-so much p-power," he muttered, clutching at his belly while his eyes glazed over. "First in... in generations."

Vesper shifted her gaze to the world beyond, eyeing the jagged stone spear protruding from the earth, cursing when she followed the complex threads of Ase holding it in place. "I don't know how to untangle this. If you pull away, it will take your innards with it."

Shoyebi coughed, bright red blood staining his lips. "Apologies... for bringing you here. We were desperate."

"Save your strength. I have little talent for healing, but I will do my best," she said, frowning in disgust as she spun the Ase from the tainted baobab into his wounds in an attempt to staunch the bleeding.

"No, too... far gone," he gasped, pushing her away. "Talented. The boy is talented but hateful. Stop him... before it's too late... for all of us."

She let out a deep breath as the spark of life faded from his eyes, her attention drawn to a violent commotion near the village. She watched as Seye vanquished the copies of herself in a torrent of flame, while battling with a group of women in red robes who acted like artillery, hurling hundreds of fist-sized rocks at the raging seeker. Vesper gasped in awe when in response his hands splayed out, her eyes losing track when countless threads of Ase erupted from his hands, grinding the onslaught of stones to dust. The women turned to flee when their attacks did nothing, and for a moment Vesper thought he would let them go, but when the women fell to the ground writhing in pain, she knew he was drawing on their life force, consuming the Ase that flowed through them.

Desperate to stop him, she touched the storm once more with her power, raising her voice high as she called to the wind, whipping her arms, turning in a circular motion until a torrent of cool air ripped down from the heavens. Seye staggered as powerful gusts of wind slammed into him, lifting him from his feet and dragging him high into the air, his compact form vanishing in the iron-gray clouds.

Vesper ran with all her enhanced speed to the fallen women, sighing in relief when she found them alive, staring at her dumbfounded. "Find as many as you can," she began, her eyes darting to clouds. "Get far away while you can."

"What's the meaning of all this?" asked one of the women as the others circled her, all of them worse for wear, their skin sagging and gray. "Has the boy finally gone mad?"

"It would appear so," she said, clutching at her head as her grip on the storm was torn away, the tornado that had thrown Seye to the sky gusting to nothing more than a soft breeze, while the temperature around them dropped quickly. "Run!" Vesper had a final view of the women in red fleeing in terror when her sight vanished after a flash of brilliant white, the deafening boom of thunder filling her ears before everything fell silent. Vesper came back to her senses with the taste of dirt in her mouth, her teeth grinding together as the bitter taste of copper filled her mouth, small arcs of electricity still coursing through her. Groaning, she sat up from the cloying earth to find the village in chaos, lightning striking among homes, black smoke filling the sky as the world around her burned.

In the distance, she caught sight of Seye entering the great split in the withered baobab, and despite the pain, she rose to her feet, wiping away beads of sweat rolling down her temples, never having felt so broken in all of her young life. Every muscle in her body burned like fire, her bones brittle, about to snap.

Vesper braced herself, straightening what was left of her shredded tunic as she took off toward the tree, her stomach turning in knots when she passed the broken bodies of men, women, and children, haphazardly flung about like forgotten toys. When she had fallen to the lightning strikes, the sour thread of Ase she was holding had dissipated, and now the tree looked sicker, with large clumps of bark falling away as she approached the crevice.

Vesper's breath caught in her throat when she entered the dark interior, the sickly-sweet odor of rotting fruit filled her nostrils. "Seye!" she called out, scanning for any sign of him. The tree looked very much the same from the interior, with strings of emerald-green light circling along the interior, except that the platforms, filled with vibrant people only hours before, were void of life, the silence deafening.

A haunting shriek from somewhere above her filled the air, and Vesper flinched back in terror when a guardian in gold-spun robes plummeted to the unyielding ground not far from where she stood, the bone-crushing impact silencing him as a pool of blood expanded beneath his broken body. Seeing no other choice, she climbed, her legs burning as she ran from platform to platform, following Seye's trail of death and destruction. The dead were everywhere she looked, with the common folk killed by simple cuts, the seeker having held his true anger for the guardians he came across. Those bodies were beyond mangled, the sum of his rage spent on breaking every bone, disfiguring each face. After an eternity of climbing, she caught sight of a flash of sunlight, not long after arriving at a final platform that led to a wide opening that looked out over the village and to the desert beyond.

Shifting her vision to the world beyond, she walked onto a narrow perch to find Seye with his arms spread wide, a myriad of threads flowing into his compact form while the skeletal branches of the baobab fell away from the dying tree. "Seye, stop this," she said, summoning her gladius, holding out the glowing blade in front of her.

"Not another step," he said. "You cannot hurt me! I hold enough Ase to burn you where you stand."

"That may be, but why hurt all of these people? I understand about Shoyebi. He was a liar, and cruel," she said, "but the rest—they're innocent?"

"Not so innocent," he said with a sneer, pointing to the branches with his chin. "My people were worse than most. Look at what they did."

Vesper had seen the writhing shades in the distance when she and Shoyebi had approached the village, but seeing them up close, her muscles turned to water as she shook with fear. "They were your enemies; they would have killed you given the chance," she said, thinking back to one of her Aunt Magda's many lessons. Her aunt had told her not to show mercy to a Sandawei warrior, that if given the chance, the kindness would not be returned.

"If it was just our enemies in these branches, the Nok would have died out long ago," he said with a bitter laugh. "No, Shoyebi and his forebears hung any who defied them in these branches."

"What?"

"Yes! Those peace-loving Berbers like Oroku, lawbreakers, any who did not follow their ways... my family included."

Vesper's stomach turned, bile catching at the back of her throat as she eyed the dead. "Your family?"

"Chosen, those strong with Ase made fine additions to this tree of horrors," he began, his smile growing when top branches fell away, both of them staggering as the tree bent back and forth. "A horror I will end today."

"Then why be a part of it for so long?" she asked. "Why not leave? We can leave now!"

Seye's form glowing a sickly green, parts of his flesh burning away. "To be what, some Roman slave like you—no. This life, these people were all I knew... until I met you."

She was taken aback, like someone had kicked her in the face. "But you hate me," she whispered, clutching at the opening as the tree swayed in the wind, the creaking of splintering wood setting her teeth on edge.

"Yes, I hated you more than you can know, but you showed me the way."

"What way?" she asked, panic setting in when more branches fell.

"You would have made a fine seeker. Most would have fled... like those cowards out there, but you, you are brave to the point of stupidity."

"What are you doing, Seye?!" she shouted as his clothes burned away, revealing an image of a baobab on his chest, similar to the one she once possessed, but bare, tainted, and twisted, with the souls of the damned lost among its branches.

"You should run... save yourself," he said, his head falling back, the glow from his body forcing her to raise a hand to shield her eyes.

Casting a quick look to those fleeing in the distance, at the bodies scattered about the burning village, Vesper pressed her lips together, knowing she was out of time. "Why do this? Why waste the time to bring me here?"

Seye's body vanished in a swarm of emerald sparks that swirled all around them, his smiling face being all that remained of his physical body. "You were the catalyst, the great hope, and my path to end this injustice. Gratitude for the end to my pain."

TWENTY
THE VOID

The tree heaved a final time, and Vesper leapt, her arms flailing as she plummeted to the rapidly approaching earth. Thinking quickly, she channeled the few threads of Ase she could grasp to spin a small cushion of air beneath her as she landed, her bones protesting as she rolled to a ball to absorb some of her momentum. "By Olodumare, what's happening," she said, coming to a halt on her back, looking up in horror of what was left of the baobab. She had expected the great tree to be falling to dust, collapsing under its own rotten weight. Instead, her legs lifted off the ground, dragged upward to a dark void that was pulling her and what was left of the village, into it.

Vesper flipped over, clawing, scraping at the burnt earth, desperate for something, anything to grasp on to. Her heart raced in terror the more the void tugged at her, and by some fluke, her hand fell on a thick root that was intact. Holding on with all her strength, she took deep, calming breaths to control her fear, knowing that panic would kill her just as quick as the debris whipping around her. Searching the horizon for those who had managed to flee, she cursed under her breath when she realized many of them had fallen and now were being dragged back despite being far away from the calamity.

Eyeing the void from the world beyond, Vesper bit her lip, seeing that Seye had somehow shattered the weave created by the Nok, releasing a torrent of Ase that collapsed into a blighted void, threatening to take her and everything else with it.

Reaching deep into the well of Ase coursing through her, Vesper delved into the ground beneath her feet, calling forth dormant seeds to sprout creeping vines that grew around her ankles, crawling up her legs to hold her in place against the unending pull of the void. Peering into the growing maelstrom, she wracked her mind for a way to escape or at least keep the destruction contained to the immediate area. The Ase on her arms took on a bright glow as she probed, sending thin weaves of power into it, only to have them ripped away by the hungry maelstrom.

Cursing in frustration, she raised her arms to try once more, only to gasp in shock when the vines binding her to the ground tore away, the tips of her toes scratching at the earth as her feet left the ground. She flailed, hunting for anything to latch on to, almost accepting that this was the end, when the tips of her fingers brushed against warm flesh. Twisting in the air, she laughed in relief. "Oroku!" she gasped, shaking her head in wonder when she saw that he was surrounded by a softly glowing sphere that floated just above the ground, shimmering like a teardrop.

"Take my hand, quickly," he said, his long, matted hair writhing like snakes.

.   .   .

He pulled her to the ground, and a tear-shaped bubble grew large enough for the both of them. "By Olodumare, where did you come from?"

The Berber was pale, with cuts and bruises covering his arms, while a jagged scrape stained his temple with dried blood. "A stone had an argument with my skull; as luck would have it, I have a hard head! I woke up moments ago to this. What happened?"

She shook her head, not really having time to explain it all. "Seye's vengeance," she said finally.

Oroku gave her a knowing look, pressing his lips into a thin line. "This was a long time coming," he shouted over the roaring wind. "After the boy's parents were cast into the baobab, he was never the same."

Vesper nodded; her eyes locked to his. "Can we use this to get us out of here?" she asked, eyeing the glowing sphere.

He shook his head, frowning up at the churning maelstrom. "I tried to pull away, but its pull was too strong. Then I saw you and thought that if we could work together, there might be a chance."

"I am not ready to die," she said, ducking to avoid her head being torn from her shoulders as debris whipped by them. "Do you know how to stop this?"

. . .

"The void is a tear in reality, impossible to fill!"

Vesper stared deep into the void, her mind burning for a solution. It looked very much like the ragged holes she had seen in the tapestry many times before, an infinite well of darkness with no end. "We must close the door, patch the hole... at least long enough that it collapses."

Oroku smiled at her, shaking his head. "It is a fine idea, but impossible. We lack the power to make it a reality."

A chill ran through her as she raised her chin, pointing to the void. "There is power in there, more than enough to do what we need to do."

"Are you mad? That is certain death!"

"It is certain death if we stay here. We must find the core of it, wall it off," she said, eyeing the glowing teardrop that was protecting them. "Can this construct keep us safe?"

"Perhaps," he said, licking his lips. "Without the baobab, I cannot draw on additional Ase, to make it stronger, but with you helping me... maybe?"

"Sometimes you have to run before you can walk," she said, taking his hand. "What are you going to do?"

· · ·

Oroku took her hand, touching it to his heart. "It is an old Berber tradition, for chosen to bond those they love to them, similar to how the Nok—"

Vesper's eyes shot open, a smile coming to her face despite the chaos around them. "I have done this... although I don't remember how.?

"Then I shall show you, so that you may know the way to keep those you love close to your heart," he said.

She watched wide eyed when Oroku opened his palm, singing a single word while making a cutting motion with his other hand. A thin line of crimson began on his open palm that he then held out to her. "This bond will be temporary and will fade with time. But can be made permanent by creating a loop as we did with the Ase weapon this morning." Vesper didn't dare blink as Oroku formed the bond between them, memorizing the intricate pattern that made her gasp in amazement when it was done. "Did you see?"

"Yes," she said, a surge of joy running through her, knowing that she could bond with Narcissus once more. "Now, let's finish this."

The tear-shaped bubble grew as Vesper combined her potential with Oroku, shimmering emerald and gold as it rose toward the collapsing void. "May the great god guide and protect us," said Oroku, when the sphere plunged into the outer edges of its dark depths, falling faster the deeper they went.

. . .

The sphere buckled, its shape bending as if a great weight were being pressed against it but still holding. "Look at that," said Vesper, her breath frosting as she spoke. Despite the pitch darkness, there were flashes of light, loose threads of emerald green swirling within invisible currents, and eddies buffeted their drop of reality. Closing her eyes, Vesper reached out with her will, gently touching at the small threads of power flickering all around her, caressing and cajoling them until she shuddered with pleasure as she filled herself with Ase, growing stronger with each passing moment while the concentric patterns on her arms and chest banished the darkness with a bright white burst of light.

"What evil is this?" whispered Oroku, his voice breaking with sadness. "So many lost to hate, for the price of arrogance! For nothing!"

A pang of sadness welled up in her chest when Vesper opened her eyes to see the destruction, the bits and pieces of lives lost from Seye's cruel genocide of his people. "We cannot change the past, Oroku," said Vesper, resting a hesitant hand on the crying Berber's shoulder, raising her head to stop her own tears from falling. "But I need you to help me, so we can stop this from happening elsewhere."

Oroku wiped his face with his tunic, nodding in agreement. "Yes, yes," he said, pointing at the debris floating just beyond their touch. "All of this, it circles like a whirlpool; we must get to the center, block it off."

. . .

They plunged deeper into the maelstrom, cutting across its axis instead of flowing with the rest of what was once the village of Ireti, Oroku drawing more Ase from her to keep the outside at bay the deeper they went. Vesper had lost track of time when in the distance she saw it, her stomach falling as she watched the ragged tear grow each time it consumed anything. "It is like I have seen in the tapestry of night," she said. "A hungry bottomless pit, its edges like rotted cloth."

"That seems accurate," he said, his breathing coming in quick, short gasps. "I hope you have a plan because we cannot go back. I have tried."

Despite the horrors around them, Vesper smiled. "I do," she said, putting a hand on his shoulder. "This... and us!"

Oroku shrunk in on himself, shooting her a terrified look. "Are you mad?"

"This construct is like all the others, pure Ase tied together in an infinite loop. It just needs to be large enough to block the whole thing."

He swallowed hard, shaking his head. "That is a very simple Idea, too simple to work."

"I have little experience with Ase, nothing compared to you and the others I met here, but I have learned that simple ideas are often the best."

"Very true," he said, his smile returning. "What do we do now?"

Vesper took his hand, squeezing hard when she felt his anxiety through their temporary bond, hoping he felt her racing heart was full of hope. "We make this construct bigger, much bigger... then we fall down the well and hope we block it up!" Oroku's brow shot up, and he squeezed her hand back when she began sending waves of Ase into their bond, their tiny sphere growing exponentially with the more power he sent into it, growing so that it was larger than the baobab that once was here, larger than the village itself.

"Wisdom and peace, peace and wisdom," he whispered as the sphere was about to touch the void, giving her one last smile before the world around them vanished to darkness, and there was nothing more.

TWENTY-ONE
THE TRIUMVIRATE

Lucilla watched in awe as the damned flooded past her, up the gravel pathway, a charging mob of souls rushing toward the domus, where she had escaped not too long ago. The moment they passed the gray-green hedge that hid the building itself, the damned began to shimmer, solidify, a rainbow of colors washing over them.

"What's happening?" she whispered as an ashen-gray-blue soul transformed before her eyes into a middle-aged centurion with a bronze chest piece, a massive hole in his chest and a tattered red legionnaire's cloak. Another one, a woman in a thin stola had skin so blistered and burned that Lucilla looked away, unable to bear the horror.

In her mind, Papa Keita's rasped in his halting Sandawei cadence: "This place is close to the world of the living. The damned reflect what they looked like just before their deaths."

She nodded as her army began to rip apart the domus brick by brick, tearing into the few servants that managed a meager resistance, men and women she recognized from her time trapped here. "Where is she?"

"The garden, the seat of her power. At the back of the domus," said Papa Keita, urging her forward.

At the mention of the garden, Lucilla's blood boiled. It was the place where she had made her greatest mistake, sealing a bargain with the Sandawei matron in a moment of weakness. She knew it was wrong, but months of living like a rat in a cage had broken her. Mother Ayaba had dangled the perfect temptation in front of her eyes, rulership of the empire she loved so much. "It is time to remove that evil woman from the field." Lucilla followed her army, the hair on her arms rising each time she looked into their eyes, in awe of the fact that from one moment they were nothing more than a shade, and the next, staring back at her with eyes that were vibrant, almost alive.

They tore through the main doors, shattering stone and wood in a storm of destruction. The old Lucilla would have been horrified to see such fine porcelain or rare furniture turned to dust, but now she was elated. Joyful, she said, "This is all part of a prison, meant to keep me forever trapped, enslaved!"

In her mind, for the first time, she heard Papa Keita laugh. It was a haunting, shrill thing and would have hurt her ears had he been in the flesh. "Pretty baubles for small minds. This is the Roman way of keeping power! Your emperors offer the people trinkets, useless gold, fool idols to worship, while they hoard the only commodity of any worth."

"Power!" shouted Lucilla, balling her hand into a fist as they strolled past the private baths, the clear water turning a brackish green with their passing, boiling with a fury that matched her raging heart. A group of shades walking alongside her shifted, taking on their living forms, that of being legionaries of high rank. Lucilla gasped when she realized the identity of one of them: an aquilifer, the legionnaire whose tall staff typically bore the golden eagle of the Roman people atop it. The very symbol that drove fear into the heart of Rome's enemies.

"Power begets power," whispered Papa Keita as the legionnaires formed a phalanx in front of her, a single clarion call from a golden trumpet sounding loud and true, calling her army to war as they exited the domus proper into Mother Ayaba's abode.

The garden was as she remembered it, filled with lush plants and trees, overgrown with the fragrances of orange blossom and jasmine almost masking the constant hint of rot wafting through the air. Lucilla was not sure what to expect, but her brow shot up for just an instant when they entered the clearing to find Mother Ayaba as she always was, sitting on a low stone bench with her hands folded on her lap, looking every bit the Roman matron she pretended to be. Lucilla took a step forward, and without a word, the matron raised her hand, and the world around her came to a halt, the ghostly legionnaires, even Lucilla herself, freezing in place, her breath catching in her throat as she struggled to breathe.

"You dare!" she the matron, glaring at her with yellow-gold eyes, the tiny beads that Lucilla knew were skulls, clicking when she shook her head. "You came to us willingly, helped us grow our power to new heights, only to throw it all away! For what? Pride? I offered you the world! Why not see it through to the end." A dry rasp escaped Lucilla's throat, and her heart raced as she fought for breath, for control. While in her mind, Papa Keita surged, whispering harsh words in his strange tongue, words that she only barely understood. Mother Ayaba watched her for a few moments longer, with the hint of a smile on her face, a smile that never touched her eyes. Finally, with a bored look, she flicked her hand. "Speak!"

"Your offer was only another cage," gasped Lucilla, clutching at her throat. "A cage that you, and only you, controlled."

"I offered you power!"

Lucilla managed to look over her shoulder as pinpricks ran up and down her arms to the bottoms of her feet. The restless dead behind her shifted, fading from shade to a living reflection, reaching out with hands hungry for life. "No one can give you power," said Lucilla, shaking her head. "It can only be taken from those who have it."

The matron narrowed her eyes, frowning at her. "Sandawei words, you've listened, and learned."

Papa Keita shifted in her mind, slithering like a snake. "Patience, she does not know I am with you. She is blind, as I was. Let her talk; vengeance is at hand."

Lucilla managed to raise her chin, looking down her nose at the Sandawei matron. "I see through your lies. You used me. Once your lapdog Magnus was no longer useful, you needed me to have Rome's senators open their doors, let their guard down so that you could steal their souls, replace them with your own people."

"Would it have been so bad? To rule the world as allies."

Her shoulders shook with laughter as she met the matron's gaze. "With your leash growing ever tighter around my neck, I don't think so. You would do with me as you did with the senators. My soul would be quickly replaced, leaving me a puppet for you to control."

Mother Ayaba shifted in her seat, her eyes narrowing at Lucilla's movements. "Your will is strong, far stronger than when you left here. Tell me, how did you survive the wastes, and how did you manage such power to call on the damned?"

"Tell her; tell her everything, except your chance encounter with me," said Papa Keita.

Lucilla cleared her throat as a warmth spread through her chest, sweat beading as the heat touched her temples. "The ritual Magnus performed, it was incomplete; when the shades touched me, they fled. With time, I learned that I could control them."

"That boy was always a half-breed fool! But you! You learned so quickly! You must have some Sandawei blood among your ancestors," she said, her eyes flashing with anger. "Or you, perhaps, you lie with the grace and skill of the Roman you are."

Lucilla tensed, every muscle stiff as steel. "The only liar here is you. I know your history, how you stole power, how—" She staggered as the ground shook, Mother Ayaba gripping tightly to the corner of her low stone bench. Even the damned behind her were careening about, searching for balance.

"What have you done, Roman?" spat the matron, her eyes darting about in wide-eyed worry.

"This is not my doing," she said, turning inward, searching through Papa Keita's mind for answers. "Is this you?"

The itan on her arms flashed a brilliant white, and Mother Ayaba shrank back, while in her mind, the old vodun roiled. "This is not me!" he said finally, panicking like a trapped animal. "This is not me!"

The shaking grew worse, and Lucilla fell, reopening the scabs on her knees, her anger suddenly trumping her fear. "Stop your lies, Ayaba. You will fall today, and none of your tricks will stop that."

Mother Ayaba opened her mouth to protest when a pulse of green light rolled over them, banishing the veil covering the garden. Mother Ayaba's low stone bench vanished, replaced by a towering throne of bone, while the garden itself vanished, leaving barren soil littered with the remains of her victims, the damned behind her reverting to ash-colored shades, wailing at the living. Lucilla gasped when she looked down at her own flesh, finding it to be pale, emaciated with the itan covering her arms appearing as bright-red, festering wounds. "What have you done to me?" she whispered, meeting the gaze of the matron, who was little more than flesh and bone.

"What is the meaning of this?" said Mother Ayaba, gazing around at the changes to the garden, her haggard face reflecting Lucilla's own confusion.

Lucilla opened her mouth to speak when the matron's eyes locked on to something over Lucilla's shoulder, her face suddenly a mask of terror. Turning on her heel, she sucked in a sharp breath at the gaping hole that stretched across the sky, a churning whirlpool of emerald green and black. "What in the name of the gods is that?" she asked, pointing.

"By Olodumare," whispered Papa Keita, shrinking back into the recess of her mind.

Mother Ayaba held on to the arms of the skeletal throne in a white-knuckled grip, her mouth twisting to an ugly snarl. "This is not our doing. What Roman treachery is this!?"

Shaking her head in denial, Lucilla fell silent, not daring to tear her eyes away when the gaping maw became like a window, the hole in the sky somehow looking out over Palatine Hill, showing the city of Rome in all its glory. A moment later, the view shifted to a burning village in the desert. She squeezed her eyes shut, thinking she was going mad, that the images would be gone when she opened her eyes, but when she looked again, she saw the sea crashing into white cliffs, looking so real that she could almost hear the cry of seabirds flocking overhead, almost taste the salty ocean air on her tongue. The swirling vortex changed again and again, almost as if it were everywhere at once, showing her places deep in the heart of Rome in one instant, and distant lands beyond her imagination the next.

Then, without warning, the void shrank, collapsing into itself while the sky bent around a now infinitesimal quivering sphere. It hung there for a moment, shaking, twisting, vibrating like a rope about to snap before suddenly exploding, sending a wave of emerald green and black that rolled toward them. Lucilla turned to run just as the wave crested over her, flowing through her with such force that she was knocked back, her entire body tingling. Lucilla came back to her senses to realize she was no longer alone with Mother Ayaba and the dead. There were hundreds, thousands of disembodied forms swirling around them, their hollow voices wailing in torment, pleading for salvation. At the heart of it all was Vesper, riding the wave across reality, her face a wide-eyed mask of panic. Not knowing how she reached out, their fingers brushing and slipping over and over again, drifting farther apart with each passing moment until with a desperate final lunge, they connected. Lucilla gasped, her breath catching in her throat as every nerve pulsed with electricity.

"Come to Rome! Find me," said Vesper, drifting away with the wave.

"How!?"

The Ose woman extended her hand, and an infinite number of

golden threads spawned from her fingers, stretching across the space between them. Lucilla tried to pull away when the amber cords touched her hands, but the Ose woman held tight. "Do not be afraid."

At the touch of the connection, a rush of adrenaline raced through her, and a deep-throated laugh poured from her throat as her heart sang with more joy than she had ever known. Where before she felt only her own beating heart, or heard the thoughts of Papa Keita, this was more. Her life, her thoughts were bound in an endless loop. She looked over to find Narcissus was somehow with them, smiling at her, then to Vesper, knowing they were all one, the song of their lives joined together. "We are a triumvirate! Three bound as one in the Roman way," she said, squeezing Vesper's hand. Vesper returned the squeeze, but before she could answer, a terrible shriek tore her from the moment, her eyes snapping forward to find Mother Ayaba charging forward to meet them.

"Caution," shouted Papa Keita in her mind, taking control.

Lucilla cringed, expecting her belly to be opened by the Sandawei matron's bone dagger. Instead, a group of ashen shades swarmed in front of her, absorbing the deadly blow. Papa Keita pressed his will, and the dead flailed at the matron, slashing, cutting, leaving deep gashes in her flesh and forcing her back.

Lucilla let go of Vesper's hand, her heart beating faster when she saw the cord between them stretch out, her connection to the Ose woman and Narcissus strong despite worlds separating them. Mother Ayaba pounced once more, streaks of crimson light spewing from the tip of her bone dagger, cutting through the damned to slam into her with the force of a hammer, spinning Lucilla on her heel and leaving an ugly welt on her shoulder. "You will not stop us! The Sandawei are everywhere!"

"She cannot hurt us, not when we are so protected," said Papa Keita, urging her on. "You are blessed by Olodumare! The damned are our strength; use them!"

Lucilla nodded, spreading her arms wide, calling the dead to her, the pulsing light on her arms glowing brighter each time one passed through her to attack the Sandawei matron. "I know your people, and I will destroy them," said Lucilla. "Just like I will destroy you." Lucilla knew nothing of the fantastic abilities Vesper and the matron possessed. Weapons were foreign to her, but she knew power, standing, and fear. In this moment, fear was the only thing in Mother Ayaba's eyes.

The Sandawei matron showed her teeth, her normally calm face twisted into a snarl. "I have lived more lives than you can imagine! But even if you best me, Magnus will soon be well in place to rule over your corrupt empire."

Lucilla raised her chin, ignoring her threats. "Your plans will be for nothing; your people will be nothing," she said, inching closer. "I know what to look for now. My triumvirate will find every Sandawei hidden in the empire, take you apart brick by brick!"

Mother Ayaba narrowed her eyes, putting both hands on the dagger. The stream of crimson grew thicker, but Lucilla felt nothing. "You are too young, too stupid to know such things!"

"Tell her now; give me her fear! Give me my vengeance!" shouted the old vodun, seething in her mind.

The Sandawei matron drew her dagger back to stab at her when they finally stood face-to-face. Lucilla only smiled when the hordes of dead circling them held tight to the other woman's arms, trapping her in place. Leaning in close, Lucilla confessed, her words coming out as a joyous whisper: "I met Papa Keita out in the wastes, and we are here to deliver his vengeance!"

"The dagger," said Papa Keita, shouting with glee in her mind. "Put it in her chest!"

"Lies!" she screeched, fighting to pull away when Lucilla pried the bone dagger from her grip, flipping it over to bury the vicious weapon deep into Mother Ayaba's heart.

"I may be too young, too stupid," said Lucilla in a harsh whisper, pursing her lips as the the matron's caramel-colored flesh blackened, bits of skin and hair burning away. "But he is ancient, and with his knowledge, I will drive your people from this world."

"No, please. I beg you," said Mother Ayaba. "Flailing against the iron grip of the damned. "Show me mercy. I know paths to power you—"

"Have you ever shown mercy?" snapped Lucilla. "Even for one day in your life?"

"No!" snarled Mother Ayaba. The last bits of her physical body began drifting away on the wind, leaving only a writhing spirit in front of her. "And I will not start today." With the last of her strength, the Sandawei matron's spirit reached deep into Lucilla's chest, catching her off guard, pulling, clawing, and tearing, sending Lucilla staggering back, clutching at nothing. They fell together in a heap, a bright flash leaving her seeing spots in the corners of her eyes, blinking in confusion. The moment only lasted for a heartbeat, and when it was over, she found herself on her hands and knees, gasping for breath, feeling empty and whole all at once. The connection with Vesper and Narcissus was still there but nothing else. Papa Keita was gone, leaving only brief flashes of himself.

Then, she heard Papa Ketia's voice, no longer in her mind, but in front of her, "Come, come, girl, no rest for the wicked."

"What happened?" she asked, clutching at her head, pushing her hair from her face. Almost falling once more when she looked up to see Papa Keita's disembodied form floating above her.

The tall vodun shrugged with his thin shoulders. "I have never seen such things in my life, but we are no longer bound. I have been replaced, and my spirit has been set free to roam among the damned."

"And the matron?"

"She was swept away, following the catalyst, the girl at the heart of the tempest... this Vesper."

Lucilla clutched at her belly, faint physical sensations coming from Vesper. They had talked about this once, not so long ago, about her bond with Narcissus, and how wonderful it would have been to have such a connection with her first husband, Verus. "She is in danger," she said suddenly. "I can feel it. Something else has found her, something to do with my brother, Commodus. She won't survive alone! I must go to her!"

Papa Keita looked over to the matron's throne of bone, his lips turning down. "Our brief connection has strengthened me, but I am more spirit than man now. I cannot leave the world of the damned now, but hopefully with time, I will find another path home," he said, his voice bitter. "But that does not mean I cannot help an ally, especially one who has given me the gift of vengeance."

"How?"

"With your strength, and the strength of your allies, we can send you home."

Lucilla looked up at him, raising a fine eyebrow. "And you—what happens to you?"

"I have waited this long. I can wait a little longer, especially if I know that my ally awaits me among the living."

She nodded, terrified of what this man could do in the world of the living, but secure that he had kept to their bargain, that he could be trusted despite his people. "I give you my word. I will find a way to bring you back. But now I must find my friend, and with her I will deliver vengeance to a common enemy, my brother."

"Blood for blood, honor for honor," he said, beginning the ritual to take her home, back to the land of the living, to whatever horrors awaited her.

TWENTY-TWO
BEASTS

The lion's sleek muscles rippled under its fur as it stalked in the shadows, the golden mane around its neck billowing in the hot afternoon breeze. A great roar echoed from the beast's deep chest as it exploded into motion, its massive paws, larger than a man's head, tearing into the sands, hunting for grip as it accelerated. The majestic animal reached the side of a large, wooden palisade, its razor-sharp claws leaving deep gashes in the wood as it scrambled for purchase, managing to climb halfway up the high wall before falling back to the sand, roaring up in frustration. The arrow pierced its deep chest below the muzzle and the Roman crowd shot from their seats, cheering, laughing, arms raised in victory as if they had murdered the beast themselves. Hapless whimpers cut through the din of the bloodthirsty crowd as the lion struggled to stay on its feet, weak growls pouring from its throat as it shambled into the shade of the tall wooden structure, its golden fur stained red as the last spark of life faded from its eyes.

"Citizens of Rome!" shouted a small man from the podium at the front of the emperor's box, the semicircular shape of the Colosseum amplifying his deep voice, so everyone could hear even over the hoots and shouts. "I give you Commodus! Imperator, Augustus, Caesar, Princeps, Dominus Noster, the slayer of a hundred lions!"

Striding along the palisade, Commodus threw his arms up in victory, basking in the adoration of the Roman people with a grandiose smile on his face. Their cheers grew, turning into gasps, when he notched another arrow, aiming at a group of senators sitting in lower tier of seats meant for those of high station. Commodus held the arrow long enough for a hush to fall over the crowd, the plebeians and slaves casting hungry looks for the blood of the highborn. The emperor let the arrow fly, the men of the senate ducking low as the arrow went wide. "Apologies, Senators," shouted Commodus, laughing with the crowd. "The light of Apollo blinded me for a moment."

"I have never been witness to such a crime," said Narcissus, crossing his arms across his massive chest, standing in the cool shade not far behind the auditor.

"He feeds the bloodlust of the people, Doctore," said Linus, the heavy iron chain around his neck rattling on the stone floor as he shifted on his low wooden bench that Commodus forced him to carry wherever he went.

"He should at least have the courage to battle the beasts on the sands, not peppering them with arrows from a distance. This is the coward's way," said the big Celt, his hands drifting to his face to rub a beard that was no longer there.

"He is here to silence his critics," said the old gladiator in a low voice, frowning as he twisted in his seat, casting hateful glances at Cleander, who was his permanent shadow. "Not that it matters; new rumors surface every day. The latest is that Commodus has lost his mind and is a drooling idiot. Taken care of by his many attendants, his wife having moved permanently to their country estates."

"The senators of Rome play a cruel game. It will be slaves and beasts that will pay the price for the emperor's anger, not them," said Narcissus as Commodus let loose another arrow, frowning when another terrible whimper of a roar reached his ear. "I have never met a man so fond of cruelty. He smiles like a child each time he kills one."

"Give me a sword and shield," shouted Commodus over his shoulder, his bronzed skin slick with sweat, glowing in the sunlight, as he adjusted the lion's mane that had become his signature. Cleander nodded to a legionnaire, and the man rushed forward, handing an ornate gladius and fine shield to the caesar of Rome. "And release the birds. I will face them on the sands to better entertain the crowd." The clang of heavy iron chains being turned, filling the air, the grinding of wood against stone shaking the Colosseum as part of the floor fell away, replaced moments later by a cage filled with large birds, each taller than a man with long necks and sharp beaks.

Narcissus bristled, shaking his head as Commodus descended the palisade with weapon in hand. "A gladius, to fight ostriches; now I have seen it all."

Linus came to his feet, cursing in pain as he stretched his bent back before shuffling forward for a better view. "This is madness," he said as the cage door flew open and a dozen of the tall birds raced out, some running away in terror, while other's shoved their beaks into the hot sand, digging holes to bury their heads in the sand despite their massive size. Commodus wasted no time, charging the ones burying their heads, chopping them off, then ripping them from the ground as the bodies flailed around him, many running headless.

"They are like the birds," said Narcissus, nodding toward the Roman patricians that filled the emperor's box, all of them clapping politely, not one of them with an ounce of empathy or sympathy for the dying animals.

"What do you mean, Doctore?"

"They bury their heads in the sand to avoid dealing with the monster living among them, praying Commodus will cut someone else's head off, never once thinking they will be next."

"A pity he has Vesper," said Linus, "else I would gladly fall on my sword to give you a chance to remove the head of that beast."

Narcissus grunted in agreement. "I spend my nights dreaming of ways to murder him," he said, glaring at the emperor with open hatred. "Of wrapping my hands around his neck and squeezing until his eyes pop from his skull." As he watched, the emperor gathered up the heads of the ostriches, striding over to where the senators sat in attendance, shaking the lifeless skulls at Rome's most powerful before finally hurling them to the ground in front of them.

"If he wasn't such an ass, it would be funny," said Linus with a laugh, his smile widening when he glanced back to see the city's high-born blanching in fear, their desire to cheer on Commodus forgotten.

"They are less than useless," said Narcissus, rolling his eyes. "Have any of the men you know in the legionary seen Vesper up close? The longer this goes on, the less confidence I have in the word of that madman."

Linus shook his head, his smile fading fast. "No, Doctore, but the woman he has shown us does have the same curve of the hip, the roundness of breast."

"I know, but—"

A burst of laughter from the crowd pulled his attention, and he looked down on the sands just as Commodus hurled the headless corpse of an ostrich among the senators, staining their fine tunics and togas blood red. "I will continue my inquiries," said Linus as the laughter died down, Commodus raising his arms in victory one last time before climbing the palisade, waving from the podium moments later, before handing his sword and shield to a waiting attendant, then returning to his seat. "Wine!" he shouted, wiping sweat from his brow. In the time it took to draw breath, an older man with a bulbous nose and long, curly hair was at the emperor's side, holding a pitcher beading with perspiration. Commodus took the cup offered by the slave, eyeing him up and down with a frown as the wine was poured. "By the gods, you're ugly."

The slave's eyes snapped open like he'd been slapped, his ears and face reddening in shame. "Apologies, Dominus." he said at last, licking his lips. "I-I don't—"

"Get this dog out of my sight," snarled Commodus, throwing his wine into the man's face, then crushing the silver cup. "And have him whipped for having the gall to come into my presence with hair like some barbarian!"

Cleander grabbed the slave roughly by his arm, pulling him with enough force that the pitcher of wine slipped from his hands, falling with a horrible metallic clatter, spilling wine over the emperor's feet. "Apologies, Dominus," shrieked the weary slave, tearing away from the Praetorian, falling to his knees to wipe away the wine with his simple tunic.

Commodus rose to his feet, towering over the quivering man. "Cleander, don't we have a few lions left? I think it's time we fed them."

"I will see to it that they are raised from the hypogeum," said the swarthy prefect, showing his perfect white teeth.

The emperor took the hapless slave by his long hair. "Disgusting," he said, dragging him out past the podium, then onto the end of the palisade, hurling him one handed onto the sands. Narcissus frowned when the man landed with the audible snap of bone, his face reddening in anger. "He did nothing wrong," whispered Narcissus out of the side of his mouth, his words meant for Linus alone.

"There is nothing we can do, Doctore," whispered Linus, his voice straining.

"He won't even have the strength to fight back," growled Narcissus, his nostrils flaring as the slave hobbled to his knees, clutching the arm he fell on.

Commodus turned in his seat, his eyes flashing a milky white for a heartbeat. "You could go down there to protect him."

"I have no fear of beasts," said Narcissus, pushing out his chin. "Only of what you would do to Linus... and Vesper."

"I am not unkind," he said. "I am a god after all. I would be entertained to see your strength put to the test. I'm sure the Roman people as well."

The sound of metal chains grinding on wood silenced the arena, followed by a distant lion's roar as a platform inched its way up from the bowels of the Colosseum. Commodus shot Narcissus one last look, and the big Celt bolted, racing down the palisade just as the lion's cage came into full view, the hungry beast spotting the downed slave, licking its chops at the sight of easy prey. He doubled his speed when the cage door swung open, his long legs matching the lion's four-legged stride as he raced to be first. The beast was almost on top of the fallen slave, its jaws stretched wide for the kill when Narcissus slammed his bulk into its flank, knocking it off course so it landed a few feet away, kicking up sand and dust as it skidded to a halt, baring its fangs.

"Can you run?" asked Narcissus over his shoulder, corralling the slave behind him while staring down the beast, not daring to look away. Eyeing the massive cat, he cursed when he saw its ribs and filthy coat, sensing that the beast had not been well tended to, even starved so that it would immediately attack whatever was placed in front of it.

"I will try, Dominus," he said, in a pain-filled whimper.

"Then run!" The lion, seeing its prey escaping, bolted, trying to race past Narcissus, only for the massive Celt to sink his meaty hands into its mane, using its momentum to swing it around, hurling the roaring beast against the wall of the Colosseum.

Against his better judgment, Narcissus turned his back, hurrying after the limping slave, lifting the man bodily as he ran past him to throw him over his shoulder. He was almost to the ladder of the wooden structure when he heard a distant roar, quickly followed by the scrape of thick claws ripping up the sand, growing louder and closer with each breath. His hand touched the first rung when instinctively he spun to his left, dodging just far enough to avoid the lion's great weight as it slammed into the wall, splintering the dry wood. The lion twisted in the air, landing with grace on all four paws.

"Apologies," said Narcissus, kicking out, landing a heavy boot to the lion's muzzle before it could recover from its missed attack. Reaching up to the highest rung, he pulled himself and the slave up, drawing his legs in close when he felt the brush of claws just beneath them. After a few moments of desperate climbing, the echo of a frustrated roar reached his ear, and he looked down to see the lion whimpering, its bony flanks heaving.

The crowd in the Colosseum broke out in cheers as he stood to his full height, many of them chanting his name, no doubt remembering his days as a champion gladiator. Narcissus felt a tug on his leg, and he looked down to see the slave hugging his leg, tears rolling down his face as his shoulders shook. "Gratitude, Dominus. I owe you my life, any—"

"I am no dominus," snarled Narcissus, pulling away from the man. "I am a Doctore, a trainer of gladiators!"

"And a warrior, worthy of praise," said Commodus, coming to stand at his side. Narcissus frowned when the emperor took his hand, raising it in victory along with himself as the crowd cheered them on.

"Praise for what, saving a fool slave who should know better?"

Commodus put an arm around his shoulder, guiding him back to the emperor's box. "You save him only to scorn him! We can throw him back if you like."

The big Celt pressed his lips together before shaking his head, frowning back at the whimpering slave who stared at him like a broken man "Look at him; he's filthy and would make a poor meal for the beasts," he said with a shrug.

The emperor threw back his head in laughter, clapping him on the shoulder. "A fine point and a fine display. Truly, you must be born of the gods! Like myself."

"Gratitude," he muttered, forcing his face to stillness, playing along in the hope that Commodus would relent and leave him in peace. "What now?"

"Now...now we enjoy the spoils of victory!" he shouted, waving one last time to the crowds as he went deeper into the emperor's box, serving himself wine from one of the many beading pitchers tucked away on corner tables.

"I will retire to my rooms, then," began Narcissus, moving to leave. Only for Commodus to shake his head vigorously.

"No!" he said, waving over a slave to pour wine for Narcissus. "Today you will drink with me, so I don't have to spend another waking moment with these weak sycophants. It will be good to spend time with another warrior, with a near equal."

"Of course... Dominus," said Narcissus, his eyes narrowing in suspicion as he sipped his wine, not liking the tart sweetness of the vintage.

"Good!" he said, turning to face the patricians, who were in attendance for today's games. "We will all retire to my chambers for some small amusements. Cleander, send someone ahead to make sure everything is to my tastes: no mistakes this time."

Narcissus groaned inwardly, hiding his anger in his cup as he took another sip. He knew very well what went on during the emperor's amusements and wanted nothing to do with them, given the last time Commodus made the offer. It was for them and them alone. Clearing his throat, he slammed his wine down on the table, meeting the other man's eyes with a hard look. "I told you before, this is not my way. My desires are only for—"

"Calm that barbarian temper," said Commodus, waving over a round-faced courtesan with wide hips and heavy breasts, whose sheer, blue stola left little to the imagination. "I know your hunger is for your Ose witch and nothing more. Marcia here will see to my pleasures."

"Very well," he grumbled, casting a weary glance at Linus before following a cheerful Commodus, who led the way to his chambers with a growing retinue of patrician sycophants following in tow.

They arrived at Commodus's vast chambers to find an army of slaves waiting for them. Young men and women with supple bodies and pretty faces circulated the many rooms, serving fine wines and offering exquisite dishes laden with exotic foods prepared to perfection, much of it still hot, the myriad of aromas making his mouth water. In every direction he turned, Narcissus found amusements.

Dancers swayed to the gentle plucks of a harpsichordist, while a pale boy with rose-painted cheeks sang a sweet ballad, his voice so perfect that some of those listening wept in open admiration.

Moving deeper into the labyrinth of rooms, Narcissus found more musicians, more dancers; the rooms were hot with the crush of bodies, more than had been with them at the Colosseum, and more arriving with each passing moment. Part of him wanted to scream at them, force them from the emperor's rooms, knowing what a monster the man was, but the longer he watched, the more he understood. The Romans who suckled at the emperor's teat ate and drank with abandon, laughing and dancing as if there were no tomorrow, living without a care in the world outside of the palace. Disgusted by all of it, Narcissus pushed through the throng, finding himself in Commodus's bath chamber, gasping for breath from the steaming water.

Wiping sweat from his brow, the big Celt caught a glimpse of the last rays of setting sun, and immediately pushed his way through the packed room to find a wide balcony overlooking a manicured garden. Cool drafts of evening air cooled him as he wandered away from the noise toward a low stone bench, his gaze drawn to winding paths, colorful statues, and bubbling fountains that dotted the area. Narcissus sighed as he sat, grateful to be alone and watch the sunset, at peace for the first time in many months. If someone had told him a year ago that he would be doctore to the emperor himself, he would have laughed in their face. Part of him knew he should be grateful for the luxuries granted to him by living in the imperial palace. His rooms were massive compared to his tiny cell at the ludus. Food, drink, women, they were all easily at hand; he wanted for nothing. Even Commodus, in his madness, appeared to enjoy the big Celt's presence, but none of it gave him a flicker of joy. For a brief, shining moment in his life, he was fulfilled, content, a free man with a woman he loved and the world laid out at his feet. Now, the wine, the food, all tasted bitter, his hatred for this life growing with each passing day. With a growl, he got to his feet, wanting to be away from Commodus and his debauchery, wishing only for his simple cell, and Vesper to go with it.

"I have ended many nights with that kind of rage beating in my chest."

Narcissus looked over his shoulder to find Commodus streaking toward him, cup in hand, wearing an open tunic and nothing more. "I-I am not angry," he began, returning his gaze to the garden.

"You don't have to lie to me," said Commodus, following his gaze. "I see it in your eyes. Those of us blessed by the divine live with the frustration, knowing that we will never find our equal. Forced to live out our lives wallowing with these lesser beings."

He kept his face still, nodding along with the ramblings of the madman, stunned that such a fool held so much power. "I do not—"

"I used to question it, you know, when I was very young," said Commodus, raising his cleft chin in a way that reminded him of Lucilla.

"What?

"My divinity," he said. "I struggled to know if I was truly blessed by Jupiter."

Narcissus narrowed his eyes, not seeing where this was going. "And now, you are certain? How?"

"It began here in my very chambers, months ago," he began, his eyes flashing a milky white, so quickly that Narcissus was sure it was his imagination. "I woke in a stupor, drunk beyond remembering, my entire guard dead around me."

He sucked in a sharp breath, cocking his head in confusion. "What kind of fool assassin would kill your men but leave you alive?"

Commodus scoffed, shaking his head. "There was no assassin. My men tried to kill me, but they failed. I still remember coming to my senses with my hands around one of their throats, watching the light fade from his eyes; it was glorious," he finished, a beaming smile on his face."

"Your own men?!" said Narcissus, looking for hints of a lie in his words, finding none. "Why would they do this?"

"Why else? Power," he said with a shrug. "Cleander's prede-cessor thought to take my head, but in his betrayal, I learned my true strength; my greatness was revealed."

"How so?" he asked, his curiosity piqued.

"When their swords shattered against my skin, when their blades could not pierce my flesh, I knew. I knew what it meant to be a god among men. But my divinity is a burden I carry every day."

"What does any of this have to do with me?"

"Because I have watched you in battle, your strength, your speed. It's all impressive. Almost as impressive as my own. I feel we are kin, both born from Jupiter himself, but I need proof, a test."

"You've seen me battle in the arena, faced me even! What more do you need?"

Commodus began to pace, rubbing his hand on the bannister of the long balcony. "I think we should repeat what happened to me," he said, turning back to face Narcissus fully. "Take every man in my rooms, every legionnaire. Kill them all, just as I did."

Narcissus frowned, his pale face flushing bright red. "I do not kill without purpose," he said, shaking his head. "To murder all those people for nothing is not my way."

"You don't do it for nothing; you do it for me," began Commodus, sneering at some of his guests who were now spilling out onto the wide balcony, falling over one another, spilling wine on the fine marble. "Look at them. They are soft, weak, a waste of life. They are not like the Romans of old. Hard men who fought and battled to build the greatest empire in the world brick by brick."

The big Celt coughed into his hand to hide his laughter. He knew little of history, but he could see. Commodus did little more than spend his days satisfying his every whim, doing much the same as the Romans he scorned. There was an audible gasp from those on the balcony; a flash of emerald green pulled his attention to the night sky. "What in the name of the gods?" he asked as a wave of roiling clouds raced toward them, jagged flashes of silent lightning cutting across the sky.

"No!" whispered Commodus, following his gaze, his body stiffening, then collapsing with a heavy groan when the roiling clouds touched him, blanketing both of them in a sickly green fog that smelled of damp, rotting wood. Blinded by the thick haze, Narcissus felt a chill run down his spine when he heard a piercing scream that put his teeth on edge. Using the wall to guide him, he half ran, half stumbled his way back to the entryway. He almost made it when another wave of screams echoed through the fog, and he staggered back as a vile odor filled his nostrils, causing him to wretch, his belly threatening to empty from nausea.

A heavy blow struck him in the chest, blasting the air from his lungs, followed by another to the bridge of his nose that left him dizzy with spots dancing in the corners of his eyes. "Face me!" he shouted, staggering as blow after blow peppered his face. With a roar, the big Celt swung his fists blindly, his powerful haymakers catching nothing but air while whatever was attacking him landed wicked blows to his nose, cheeks, and throat, leaving him breathless. Changing tactics, he tightened up, pulling his arms close in front of him to protect his face while lashing out with his knees and elbows in hopes of catching his attacker off guard. In response, he found himself lifted bodily, slammed against the wall with enough force that his body fell limp, coughing up bright blood from his lungs as he slumped to his haunches. Pushing his back against the wall, he tried to stand, only to be knocked back by the invisible force.

"Finish it!" he said, his breath coming in heavy gasps.

The force battling him drew back, and he looked up, intending to face whatever was about to kill him, when suddenly the clinging fog was blasted away, revealing a titan-sized shadow in the shape of a man, only visible by the light it blocked. Narcissus gasped when behind it the sky was dominated by a whirling void that stretched from east to west, images of places beyond imagining rippling across its surface, shifting and changing with every breath. The shadow stopped its killing blow to follow his gaze, a defiant screech piercing his ear as the creature recoiled, shrinking in on itself. The big Celt blinked, and suddenly the infinite void shrank down to a small point in the sky, the stars returning to their rightful place in the sky.

The creature let out a triumphant shriek when the void vanished, raising its shadowy fists to finish Narcissus for good.

The blow was about to land when a web of golden threads spun into place in front of the creature's fist, halting the attack. Narcissus let out a breath, his shoulders slumping in relief as the creature kicked and screamed as it was dragged away from him, over the balcony and into the garden, vanishing in the darkness. The clinging fog began to clear, and he frowned when he saw a thin cord of shadow stretching away from Commodus, snaking into the garden, toward where the creature had vanished. Narcissus wanted nothing more than to sit, close his eyes, and lay back against the wall until the pain went away, but something nagged at him, and his breath caught in his throat when he realized there was no music, no underlying din of conversation, only an oppressive silence that worried him. He pushed back against the wall to stand, his eyes narrowing when he glanced into Commodus's chambers. Everyone, every last sycophant from Commodus's retinue, was comatose, or dead.

Narcissus was about to enter when a flickering amber thread shot from the garden, darting toward him. He turned to run, only to curse in frustration when the cord wrapped around his wrist, locking his arm in place as more threads emerged, taking only a heartbeat to wrap him in a glowing web from head to toe. A rasping gasp poured from his throat when an icy wave washed over him, healing the bruises on his face, his breath frosting as the same coolness pierced his lungs, easing the pain in his chest. Narcissus smiled when a familiar connection settled on his shoulders, and a world of sensation that he had almost forgotten, returned to him, completing him. He blinked, and she was there, floating over the railing of the balcony with a glowing bubble that enveloped them, blocking out everything, giving him the feeling that they were the only people in the world. He looked into her dark eyes, drank in her brilliant smile, falling in love once more, with the curve of her lips "I thought I'd lost you."

"Never! " she whispered, giggling as she touched the naked flesh where his beard once was, her eyes saying all that needed to be said. "Are you well, my love?"

The screech of the shadow called his attention, and the terror-filled shouts of panicked Romans made him wince, but none of it mattered; none of it frightened him. "I am," he said with a short nod. "You?"

She nodded, kissing him despite the chaos flowing around them. "I am."

"What now?" he said, his smile growing wider.

Vesper shrugged, glancing around. "Now, now we save these fools from themselves!"

TWENTY-THREE
HERAKUN

An ear-piercing shriek shattered the silence, the balcony tilting as the garden heaved, earth and stone spewing high into the air to shower debris onto the barrier she had created. "We have to move!" she said, pulling her lips away with a pang of regret, wishing she and Narcissus had shared more than just a fleeting moment.

"What's going on?" he asked as he stood to his full height.

Vesper began to answer when a sphere of pure Ase emerged from the darkness of the garden, Oroku meeting her eyes with a look of terror on his pointed face. "It's a long story," she began, looking up at the towering shadow on the berber's heels, the monster tearing away the last remnants of the amber net she had crafted to restrain it. "But let's just say that for a moment our world, and the worlds beyond, were one. Every spirit, every loa in our reality was drawn toward the void where they truly belong, breaking any bonds they had to the flesh.

"Commodus?" asked Narcissus, his eyes once more drawn to the filament of shadow connecting the emperor to the shadow descending upon them.

Oroku was on them suddenly, his sphere of golden amber enveloping them, shielding them just in time against the shadow's titanic attack. Vesper flinched, eyeing the cracks forming and then vanishing with each blow. "We suspected since the battle with Saoturus that something was going on with him," she said, the ashe on her arms flashing bright as she took the berber's hand, adding her strength to their shield. "But nothing like this. I have never seen a loa so powerful." She gritted her teeth, bracing for another of the shadow's attacks, only to narrow her eyes in confusion when the creature moved past them, plunging deep into the emperor's chambers and spreading out, the rooms barely visible behind a darkened haze.

"What's it doing?" asked Narcissus when the shadow descended on the fallen bodies.

Vesper began to shake her head, only to suddenly gag when a fetid odor touched her nose, her stomach heaving as her eyes watered from the smell. "By Olodumare! It's hunting for easier prey," she whispered, her voice full of horror as the bodies fell apart, melting like wax, until only putrid pools of dark liquid remained. "It was him!"

Narcissus blanched, nodding hard. "The incidents, the ones we investigated with Lucilla. Was it Commodus all along?"

"I think so," said Vesper, remembering the smells, the vanished bodies. The scenes of madness they had witnessed over the last year, most of them a mirror to the one happening in front of them. "O-or, or at least part of it."

Oroku bent in half, retching with violent heaves until nothing else came out. "What creature of nightmare is this?" he said, wiping his mouth on his sleeve as the sphere backed away when the shadow spilled once more onto the balcony, creeping ever so slowly toward the emperor's inert form.

"Do we let it kill him?" asked Narcissus, taking her hand in his.

Vesper eyed the shadowy cord connecting Commodus to the creature as it drew closer to him. "Look at it," she said, wrinkling her nose when torrents of red and black rippled up and down its form, which was now thicker, slower. Giving it the appearance of a beast that had eaten its fill. "I don't think it means to kill him. It looks... satisfied, like it's returning home."

"You mean it is bonded with him? Joined to his flesh?" asked Narcissus.

"There are stories," began Oroku, his voice trembling, "of ancient loa who hide in the world, living life after life, fueling their power with the Ase of mortals."

"Then let Rome reap what it has sown," said Narcissus. "I have suffered enough for this empire, given up too much. I'm done."

Vesper pressed her lips together, torn between her sense of duty to protect life, to keep to the pact made long ago between the Ose and Rome... but Commodus was a monster, a cruel man who took pleasure in the pain of others, herself included. "He has the blood of my people on his hands, and I'm tired of protecting a man who, in his ignorance, broke a pact that protected Rome from the very thing consuming him now. I can do better for the world far away from him. Let Commodus deal with the mess he has created." She was about to direct Oroku to take them away from the palace and the city itself when Commodus bound to his feet, scrambling away from the stalking shadow, his eyes wide with fear.

"Get back, beast. Do you know who I am! Caesar of Rome! Son of Jupiter. You cannot have me!"

The stalking shadow came to a halt, the edges of its shape warping, twisting in ways that made Vesper's stomach bubble with fear. "You are nothing without me," said the shadow, its voice a piercing needle in her ear. "You wished to be a god. I have made you a god."

"Not like this," pleaded Commodus, falling on his haunches and raising his hands defensively as the creature came closer, the cord connecting them growing thicker. "Not trapped in the bowels of my own mind... a prisoner."

"Coward," muttered Narcissus, frowning like he'd eaten something bitter.

A whiff of death drifted from Commodus's chambers, forcing

Vesper to once again look at the carnage, eyeing the pools of black liquid left by the creature. It was clear from the creature's bloated appearance that it was satiated for now, but given time, it would be hungry again, and with Commodus as its puppet, who knows what could happen. "This is only the beginning. The killing will continue if we leave," said Vesper at last, bowing her head while she clenched her fists. "At the very least, we have to stop that thing from rejoining him. Stop it, here, now!"

Through their reformed bond, she felt Narcissus bristle with rage, his blood burning hot. "No!" he shouted, shaking his head. "I have just gotten you back! We have sacrificed too much, paid too high a price. We can leave Rome to burn for all I care!"

Vesper touched the stars on her shoulder blades, reaching deep inside her, finding the small spark that connected her to the primordial loa that had marked her so. "I'm sorry," she said, meeting his angry gaze at last. "I must be better than my enemies, lest I become them."

Her heart skipped a beat when his grip on her hand weakened, and he started to pull away, his face flushing a deep red. It only lasted a moment, but it was long enough to leave her weak in the knees, terrified that she had pushed him away. "Can you stop this thing," he said finally, his grip solidifying, unyielding.

"Yes, but not without help."

"Then we will face it together," said Narcissus, flexing his massive arms.

"No, my love, this battle will be beyond the physical, and I don't want to lose you... ever again," she said, pushing him away. "Oroku. Take him far away from here. Now!"

The berber nodded, never blinking. "Peace from wisdom, wisdom from peace."

"No!" shouted Narcissus as she leapt, his growling protests fading as Oroku's sphere sped off, vanishing into the night.

The shadow was almost on top of Commodus when Vesper

landed on the heaving balcony, the beast coming to a halt, a predator sniffing the air when new prey arrived, then snapping around to extend its hungry claws toward her. A storm of light erupted from her chest as she channeled the Ase in her blood through the stars decorating her neck, while words of power poured from her throat: "Eshu, son of Olodumare, master deceiver. I call upon you for a simple task. Give me your power so that I may destroy our enemies. In return, I offer my blood! My service, my life."

The shadow creeping toward her froze in place at the mention of Eshu, its form bending back on itself while shades of crimson flashed across its surface. "You summon the deceiver," it whispered, Vesper wincing from its piercing voice. "You are a fool! I will offer you a quick death so that you do not have to suffer under his cruelty." The creature pushed through the bursts of light pulsing from the stars on her collar, the putrid shadow contorting, deforming with each step it took toward her.

Vesper shuddered as she felt Eshu descend upon her, the primordial loa's spirit pouring into her body with such force that she staggered from the power racing through her blood, while the tattoos across her chest erupted in a brilliant cascade of light. In the past when she had shared her body with Lillith or Papa Jufari, it had been a battle of wills to control her body, a battle she had often come close to losing as the loa fought to push her out. This was different. Instead of dominating the spirit and forcing it to her will, it was like she had opened a door to find a friend waiting for her, both of them sharing a space. Eshu's potential adding to her own.

"A simple task!" shouted Eshu in her mind as he settled into her body, drinking in the world through her senses, her eyes snapping open and her jaw falling when he saw the bloated shadow pouring into Commodus.

"You didn't answer last time, so I made it... sound simple."

"You tricked me!" said the loa in her mind, his thoughts full of anger, then shifting to amusement. "Good!"

Vesper smiled when a concentric pattern on her arm came to life, forming the gladius of light she had crafted, blazing like the noonday sun as it appeared in her hand. "Now look at what we face," said Eshu as she began to tremble when the barrier between the primordial loa and herself blurred, gasping as ancient wisdom poured into her mind. Knowledge stretching back to the creation of time, the weave itself. Together they were witness to the creation of the loa joined with Commodus, a twisted afterbirth of the first servants created by Olodumare, meant to be left to wither and die, only to live on as a parasite, attaching itself to the most hateful and savage of the first peoples, hiding in the world, growing in power with each new connection, building and growing for millennia until it became a creature of legend, summoned by the foolish.

"Eshu, how do we stop a creature that old, that powerful," she said, swallowing hard.

The trickster loa smiled with her face, shrugging her shoulders. "We cannot kill it, but we can send it back beyond the void, far away from this world: we only have to control it for a moment."

The shadow had almost completely joined with Commodus, with only a few writhing threads of shadow flickering around him when she stepped forward, calling it out in bold tones. "Herakun the mighty, lord of shadows. I call on you!" she began, her voice a mixture of Eshu's and her own, booming with a powerful cadence that echoed across the garden and beyond. "Give me your power, your strength so that I can vanquish my enemies!"

At the powerful call, Commodus staggered forward, falling on his face as the ancient loa Herakun was ripped from his body, the bloated shadow now towering over her, its trembling form growing with each passing moment. "You dare!" it echoed in a hollow voice that vibrated through her, shaking her to the core of her being.

"I command—"

"You command nothing," it shouted, surging forward to try and envelop her. "I am ancient, beyond your understanding, beyond the strength of the pathetic loa riding your bones."

The shadow washed over her, and Vesper's flesh stung, burning and freezing all at once, her eyes blurring from the pain. In response, Vesper pulled hard on Eshu's strength, sending more Ase coursing through the blade. Night turned to day as she raised her gladius high, leaving her blind, blinking away spots as the weapon flared with torrents of amber light that cut large swaths of shadow from Herakun, forcing it to bend back over on itself. "I command you!" it said again.

"You. Command. Nothing!" roared the twisted loa as it surged forward, screeching, screaming, howling as bits and pieces of it tore away while it charged toward her. Vesper blinked, and she found herself enveloped in a vortex of darkness, Herakun's corruption burning away her flesh, boiling her blood, while Eshu's strength healed her, patches of newly grown flesh appearing as quickly as it vanished.

"I... I... can't hold it," she whimpered, gritting her teeth while she fought for breath, wanting nothing more than to give up, drift away on the wind and find peace, but somehow holding on.

"You must hold on, for both our sakes," screamed Eshu in her mind, giving Vesper every ounce of his strength.

Vesper nodded, using every shred of Ase she had, cursing each time the scale of life and death slipped in favor of Herakun, with more of her burning away while she faded toward oblivion, "How do we... How do we return it to the void, to the world beyond?"

"A gate!" said Eshu, his words strained. "A way back to the void where he belongs."

Vesper closed her eyes, feeling for the connection she had just made, the connection she intended to use to find her friend. "Lucilla, I need you. The words had barely left her mouth when she felt a sudden rush of closeness, a web of connection that eased her pain, tipping the scales once more into balance against the wicked shadow. The air in front of her shimmered, a violent tear splitting the illusion of reality open to reveal a bone-strewn garden filled with dull green-gray plants, Vesper gawking in amazement when she saw Lucilla step into view.

The noble woman looked nothing like she remembered. Her face was a mess of scars while her long, brown hair, once perfectly coiffed like a crown, hung past her shoulders, ragged and filthy like the filthy stola she wore. Most shocking, her once pale skin was now covered in the twisted symbols used by the Sandawei, the flesh on her arms red and festering from wounds never given time to heal. "Keep the portal open," she said over her shoulder as she stepped from the portal to take Vesper's hand, squeezing hard.

"Are you well?" she asked, worried for her despite matching her will to Herakun's.

"Take what little strength I have," said Lucilla, her voice cracked and broken, the portal behind her beginning to close.

Vesper nodded, pushing Lucilla behind her as she redoubled her efforts, blasting beams of light into the shadow, Herakun's screams shaking the foundations of the great palace. "I command you to return to the void, to face—"

Herakun fell back, its warped form fighting against every step Vesper took toward it. "You will not win," it said, turning to flee. "I will find another sack of flesh."

The force resisting Vesper relented, and for a moment she panicked. "I cannot let... you... leave," she said, plunging her blade deep into the fleeing loa, the threads of light from the weapon spreading out through its form, burrowing deep into the chaos that held it together.

A dark filament shot from Herakun's fading form, burying itself deep into Commodus, using the caesar of Rome to drag itself forward, pulling Vesper with it. "You have lost, Ose witch," shouted Herakun as it dove toward Commodus.

"Keita! Take him."

Vesper ignored the shout and lunged, trying to stop it, but something pushed her aside, sending her tumbling. She looked up to find the bloody symbols on Lucilla's arms glowing a bright white blue as she somehow managed to push the shadow into the portal, a pair of long arms from the other side pulling the loa the rest of the way in. Vesper shook her head, narrowing her eyes as the portal snapped shut, the world around them falling silent. "What... How.... how did you?"

Lucilla glided over to her, falling cross-legged beside her. "Apologies. I did not mean to hurt you."

Despite every fiber of her body stinging with pain, Vesper fell back against the wall and laughed, while in her mind, Eshu did the same. "Hurt me? You saved me," she said, glancing over at Commodus. "Your brother too."

The noblewoman glanced over at Commodus, raising her chin. "A mistake I intend to fix," she began, pushing herself up using the wall. "Vesper... can you make a gladius?"

Vesper's eyes drifted between the siblings, a chill running through her when she saw the hatred in her friend's eyes. "Of course," she said, pulling together the threads of Ase to conjure a simple steel gladius for her.

Lucilla pressed her lips together when the blade appeared in her hands. A fierce snarl escaped her throat when she drifted to stand over her brother. "He did this to me, you know," she said in a flat tone. "Imprisoned me, starved me until I was forced to make the worst bargain of my life. It only got worse from there."

"End it quickly, and let us begone from this place," said Vesper rubbing her arms. "Everything about this is putting my nerves on edge."

"For my husband, for our father," began Lucilla, raising the gladius over her head, the point of the weapon aimed at her brother's chest.

"Wait!" shouted Eshu with Vesper's voice, his words a mix of terror and panic as he reached out to stop Lucilla.

Lucilla staggered, gasping in shock as she clutched at her chest. "What!?"

The gladius in Lucilla's hands faded as Eshu took control of Vesper, unraveling the weave holding the blade together. "What is the meaning of this?" said Vesper, appearing as if she were talking to herself.

In her mind, Eshu shifted, adjusting, preparing for battle. "Look, truly look," he whispered, pouring Ase through Vesper, hardening her skin, making her muscles steel.

"Talk to me; what in the name of the gods is going on?" asked Lucilla, her cheeks reddening as if she'd been slapped.

Vesper raised a hand to silence her, trying to make sense of the jumble of thoughts racing through her mind. Finally, she calmed her racing heart and did what she was told, shifting her vision to the world of the spirit, of the weave. "By Olodumare," she said, stumbling back.

"What?"

"Herakun, it's still there," said Vesper, cocking her head as she stared. "Or at least still connected to him somehow." A thick cord of shadow stretched out from Commodus, vanishing a few feet later. Making Commodus appear to be a marionette, dancing on some puppeteer's string.

"A fine trick," said Eshu with Vesper's voice, walking around Commodus to inspect the dark connection. "If we cut the cord, it will resummon the beast, tearing a hole in our world to let it run free, unrestrained by the physical. A nightmare for the world."

"What do we do?" asked Vesper, resting a hand on Lucilla's shoulder while the other woman began to sob, her body shaking as she slumped to her knees.

"As long as this fool lives, Herakun is locked away," said Eshu, speaking in her mind now, his words for her alone. "But the moment he dies, the world will suffer as the dark loa tries to consume it all to grow its power. So it would seem you have no choice."

Vesper shook her head, pressing her lips together. "No!" she said, pacing back and forth, the weight of what she had to do pressing hard on her shoulder.

Lucilla gave her a questioning look. "What?"

She stopped, looking up at the stars, taking in a deep breath. "For the moment, we have to keep your brother safe. If he dies, the beast goes free to ravage, to feed, and the world will look like the chambers behind us."

"No," she whispered, shaking her head.

"Until the time comes, we must be a shield to Commodus. Keep him safe, no matter the cost, or the world will die with him."

EPILOGUE

Magnus wandered the shattered remains of the garden, cursing with each step, his jaw hanging open in awe at the destruction. When Mother Ayaba had ordered him to Rome with the task of organizing the senators they controlled, the last thing he expected was to return home to find the Sandawei matron gone, with their home in ruins. Delving deeper into the garden, it was clear a great battle had taken place here, how, he could not imagine. Their stronghold here was meant to be invincible against living armies.

Arriving at the heart of the garden, his brow shot up in shock when he saw the illusion of Mother Ayaba's simple bench was gone, her towering stone throne visible for all to see. He removed his red-painted mask, letting the garish skull clatter to the stone path while he reached down to find the matron's Obe, the bone dagger that was a powerful tool in channeling her power, but more importantly, it was a symbol of her dominance of the Sandawei people. Magnus smiled to himself when he ripped off his toga and then the tunic beneath, exposing his skinny chest. "Blood for power, power for blood," he repeated over and over, not hesitating as he cut deep gashes over his heart, the bone dagger drinking it all in, not a single drop falling to the ground.

When he was done, he plunged the dagger in his belly, a shout of triumph escaping his lips despite the piercing agony. The hurt only lasted a moment, subsiding with each breath, until finally the blade slid from his stomach, his pale flesh whole and untouched. Bounding to his feet, he could already feel the changes, amazed at how light he felt, like he had put down a great weight that he had been carrying for his whole life, relishing in his newfound strength. His vision was the strangest, and when he looked out, he could see back and forth along the weave, and if he focused, could catch glimpses of the living world even at the heart of Rome itself despite, or due to, the corruption that engulfed the city: he couldn't be sure.

Pushing it all from his mind, he mounted the steps to the throne, trembling as a rush of sensation threatened to overwhelm him when he sat. Touches of flesh on flesh smell fantastic and foul, words spoken in languages foreign and familiar caressing his ear as connections to the other Sandawei stretched across the world reached him. Gripping the arms of the throne, he cleared his throat, speaking in a powerful voice that reached all of the first people hidden throughout the world. "Hear me, brothers and sisters!" he began, his blood racing with each word. "I, Magnus, chief vodun of the Sandawei, call for you to pledge your blood, your life, your loyalty! Now and forever, until the true death!"

Magnus smiled, leaning back on his throne as their words came to him, his power growing with each pledge, with each oath. He would rule the Sandawei now and finally bring his people into the light, to rule not only Rome, but the world.

The End.

. . .

Vesper Will Return.

ALSO BY RHETT GERVAIS

Pre-order today!

Invictus: The Last Witch of Rome: Book Four

DID YOU ENJOY THIS BOOK? YOU CAN MAKE A HUGE DIFFERENCE

Reviews are the most powerful tool in my arsenal when it comes to getting attention for my books. As much as I'd like to, I don't have the muscle of a New York publisher. I can't take out full page ads in the newspaper.

Honest reviews of my books help bring them to the attention of other readers.

If you've enjoyed this book I would be very grateful if you could spend just five minutes leaving a review (It can be as short as you like) on the book's page. You can jump to the page by clicking on the link below.

Imperator: The Last Witch of Rome: Book Three

ABOUT THE AUTHOR

Rhett's love for all things science fiction grew out of a Sunday morning family tradition of watching Star Trek re-runs on the CBC. His love of storytelling is the result of too many hours as a dungeon master trying to murder his players!

He lives in Pincourt Canada with his wife, daughter, and a crazy calico named Maggie.

www.ingramcontent.com/pod-product-compliance
Lightning Source LLC
Chambersburg PA
CBHW031426200626
46814CB00016B/2492